# The Shaman Stone

**A multicultural mystery of supernatural proportions**

*May the Shaman Stone transport you to adventure and new understandings. Enjoy the journey.*

*June Gossler Anderson*

## June Gossler Anderson

Grannygirl Press

June Gossler Anderson

Copyright 2010   June Gossler Anderson

Published by Grannygirl Press
Andover, Minnesota

All rights reserved. No part of this book may be reproduced or transmitted in any form or by any means, electronic or mechanical, including photocopying, recording, or by any information storage and retrieval system without written permission from the author, except for the inclusion of brief quotations in a review.

ISBN: 9780984488506
LCCN: 2010922968

All characters in this book are products of the author's imagination. Any resemblance to persons living or dead is purely coincidental.

Cover art: Caryn Inderlee
Cover graphics: Ryan Dawson
Interior design: Todd Anderson


Printed in the United States of America

# The Shaman Stone

*for Roger*
*friend, husband, and research buddy*
*We shared the adventure.*

June Gossler Anderson

**Acknowledgements**

Although this book started out as pure fiction, I was drawn into the possibilities presented by combining fact with fiction. My years of research took me to many written sources of information, and provided me with people to talk with, and places to visit. They are listed in the bibliography at the end of the book.

I would especially like to thank Michael Budak, author of *Grand Mound*, published by the Minnesota Historical Society Press, for his invaluable information about this largest of Minnesota Indian burial mounds located west of International Falls, and his recounting of the reburial of ancient Indian bones; and our wonderful guide, Sherry Wilson, at Kay-Nah-Chi-Wah-Nung Historical Center, The Place of the Long Rapids, across the Rainy River in Stratton, Ontario, Canada. Her personalized in-depth guided tour of those burial mounds provided much information and insight into the lives and burial customs of these early peoples.

I am also indebted to Ker Lor for sharing her painful story of loss and escape from Laos in the aftermath of the Vietnam War thirty years ago. I had originally asked her to verify my facts about the Hmong culture and check out the escape story I had already written to see it if was "over the top." She nodded her head as she read and said, "Yes, it was believable;" then she told me *her* story. My version of the escape paled in comparison and I asked if I could incorporate her account into mine.

# The Shaman Stone

A special thank you to my granddaughter, namesake, and soccer player extraordinaire, Taylor June Anderson, who wrote the play by play description of the soccer game in Chapter 22.

I would also like to thank my writing groups, Sandhill Writers in Bethel, Coon Rapids Writers, and Northwords/Rice Creek Writers at Banfill Locke Center for the Arts for patiently listening to my story, chapter by chapter, month after month, and offering encouragement and suggestions. A big thank-you to Shirley Christenson, Linda White, and Anya Anderson for their insights, thoughtful advice, and helpful suggestions.

A hug of gratitude to my sister, Gail Kishish, who did the final proofing with her usual meticulous eye for errant words and letters; to Caryn Inderlee, an artist of extraordinary talent who created the cover art; to Ryan Dawson who designed the graphics for that cover; and to my son, Todd Anderson, for the interior layout and design.

Most of all, I would like to thank my husband, Roger, for accompanying me on my research missions and "loving" the book as I was writing it. I only wish he had lived to read it in its final form.

June Gossler Anderson

**About this book**

The State of Minnesota is unique in that it has a large Indian population, the second largest group of Hmong immigrants in the nation, and once housed over eleven thousand Indian burial mounds. It is upon these elements *The Shaman Stone* is based.

*The Shaman Stone* is set in the 1980s, in the aftermath of the Vietnam conflict, when many Hmong people were relocating in the United States. Their stories of fleeing from the Pathet Laos to settlements in the United States, as related in this book, are from actual accounts.

Although this book is a work of fiction the descriptions of shamans, burial mounds, and migration of the first people to the Americas during the last Ice Age are based on archaeological and anthropological evidence even though these findings are not always in accordance with the belief systems of some modern day Indian tribes. The inclusion of the Shaman Stone, time and space travel, and the bone and stone legend are, of course, fictional devices used to advance the story.

Throughout the book I use "Indian" in preference to the politically correct term, "Native American," which was not in vogue in the 1980s. I also defer to the logic of the Smithsonian's American Indian Museum in Washington DC which states that *anyone born in the Americas, including Hawaii, is a "Native American."*

Between 25,000 and 8,000 years ago the 50 mile waterway called the Bering Strait, separating Alaska from Siberia, was high and dry, locked up in massive ice sheets that covered about one-third of the Earth's surface. It is generally agreed that the peopling of the Americas began when hunters from Siberia followed big game animals across a broad stretch of tundra to Alaska. (We now call this flooded land bridge "Beringia.") Once the glaciers receded and ice corridors opened, these ancestral Indians continued their migration, fanning out as far south as the tip of South America, and east to the eastern seaboard of the US, and Greenland beyond.

Shamanism, a main theme of this book, is defined as "a range of traditional beliefs and practices that are concerned with communication with the spirit world and claim the ability to diagnose and cure human suffering." (Wikipedia) According to Grim, "Among tribal peoples the shaman is the person, male or female, who experiences, absorbs, and communicates a special mode of sustaining, healing power." (*The Shaman* p.3) Of shamans, *National Geographic* says, "Religious leaders--often called medicine men because their activities included curing the sick--wielded great influence through their communication with the spirits." (*World of the American Indian*, p. 121)

Mounds in uncounted thousands sprinkled the eastern part of the United States. Burial mounds of the Adena culture in Ohio and Kentucky date back to about 1000 B.C. They contain well-made pottery, ornate art objects, jewelry, and tubular smoking pipes of stone. The Adena was followed a few centuries later by the Hopewell, an agricultural society of mound builders who produced elaborate log tombs full of rich offerings of pottery, stone carvings, and art objects of copper, shell and mica. Some of the raw materials came from as far away as Yellowstone, the Gulf of Mexico, and the Great Lakes area, indicating a vast trading network.

The Temple Mound Period, lasting nearly 1000 years, began about 700 AD with the Mississippian peoples who raised huge pyramidal hills, usually around a central plaza, with temples on the flat summits. The largest of all temple complexes rises in Cahokia in western Illinois. Its central mound towers 100 feet in height with a base covering some 16 acres. It is the site of the world's largest serpent effigy, a coiled quarter-mile of heaped earth.

More modest in size were the approximately 11,000 burial mounds that once dotted the landscape of Minnesota. Included among them are the Laurel Mounds of northern Minnesota dating from 2,200 years ago. The most notable of them is Grand Mound, west of International Falls on the Rainy River, and an array of mounds at Kay-Nah-Chi-Wah-Nung, <u>The Place of the Long Rapids</u>, in Stratton, Ontario on the other side of the Rainy River in Canada. Although their location is purposely ambiguous in *The Shaman Stone*, it is these mounds upon which my story is based.

# The Shaman Stone

## June Gossler Anderson

*I didn't know if it was a voice in my head that woke me or if I actually heard one. The early morning sun was blasting in through my bedroom window, and a bunch of birds were squawking like mad. One big bird in particular really freaked me out. It was sitting on my mother's grave staring at me through the window. It was an eagle.*

# 1
# Maggie Falls

Dad threw the thunderbolt during dinner. We were sitting around the table, Dad, Aunt Betty and me. His fork, loaded with roast beef dripping with gravy, was halfway to his mouth when he said, "By the way, we're moving back into town," just as casually as if he were telling us it was going to rain tomorrow.

Aunt Betty was so startled by Dad's announcement that her spoon missed her mouth and the mashed potatoes balancing in the bowl end landed in her lap. "What are you talking about, brother!" she exclaimed. "Who's going to manage the cemetery if we move to town?"

Dad swallowed his roast beef, took a swig of coffee, and said, "You will, Betty. You know the ropes. Radcliff & Sons needs me in town full time. *You* are staying here. Elizabeth Mae and *I* are moving to town."

"Staying here? All by myself?" Aunt Betty looked like she had been struck by lightning.

"No way!" I yelled. "You can move to town by yourself. I'm staying right here with Aunt Betty!"

## June Gossler Anderson

Dad set down his coffee cup and fixed us with his steely gray-eyed glare. "Aunt Betty's a big girl, Elizabeth Mae, and so are you. Now that she will be managing the cemetery full time, without me telling her what to do, she won't have time to be your babysitter as well. You're starting junior high this year. It's time you started hanging around with some kids your own age."

"Those stuck-up town kids! I'd rather pitch a tent in the cemetery and make friends with the ghouls."

"Don't be ridiculous, Elizabeth Mae. You'll find your friends in seventh grade, not the graveyard, and it's about time you did." Dad put his fork on his plate, pushed out his chair and left the table. I was sitting by myself. Aunt Betty had already stormed up to her room.

Dad, Aunt Betty, and I had lived in the old family house next to the cemetery ever since I could remember, almost thirteen years now. My mother died when I was born. I don't remember her at all. I only know her from her pictures. Aunt Betty, who is twice my age, is my dad's younger sister but there is no family resemblance. Dad is tall, dark-haired like me, and muscular. (I think it's from carrying all those coffins.) Aunt Betty is small with long blond hair that she usually wears in a ponytail. When Grandma and Grandpa Radcliff passed away Dad rented out our home in town and we moved into the cemetery house with Aunt Betty so we could all take care of each other. It was a happy arrangement for me since Aunt Betty had become not only my substitute mother, but also my best friend. And now Dad was going to ruin it all.

No way did I want to move into town. People there say I have a morbid personality. That's probably because I was brought up in the Maggie Falls Cemetery and my dad is the town's undertaker. "Radcliff & Sons, Morticians" the sign reads. I'm not one of the sons. I am his only daughter, Elizabeth Mae Radcliff, named after my Aunt Betty.

Actually, Dad is the only Radcliff son left to carry on the business. Aunt Betty says the town of Maggie Falls, Minnesota used to be full of Radcliffs, but now there are more Radcliffs buried in the Maggie Falls Cemetery than living in the town of Maggie Falls.

We Radcliffs, or what's left of us, have been here for a long time. As soon as the Indians signed the treaty turning their land over to the United States government, Great-great-great-grandfather Henry Radcliff bought himself a covered wagon, filled it with his woodworking tools and his new wife and joined his neighbors for the long trek west to Minnesota territory from their homes in New England. They set up housekeeping on the Indian River just below the spot where Rice Creek pours into it over a baby-sized waterfall. The river and the creek already had a name; the waterfall did not, so when my great-great-grandmother Margaret Radcliff was born, they named it Maggie Falls in her honor since she was the first white child born in the new town, which they also named Maggie Falls. How do I know all this? It's right here in the book my Aunt Betty wrote. Its title is *A History of Maggie Falls, Minnesota; 1850-1980.*

After its publication last year, Aunt Betty became the Toast of The Town--a regular celebrity. Not only was she asked to join the Founding Families of Maggie Falls (FFMF), they made her its president, a position that is usually held by the banker's wife, or the doctor's wife, or some other equally important personage. So now Aunt Betty is busy digging into the rest of her past, trying to find some important ancestors.

Dad kept his word. A few weeks before school started we moved into our "stately old house" (Dad's description) on Third Avenue West. It was built around the turn of the century in the best part of town by people who had money and fancy titles like "Doctor," "Lawyer," "Judge," and "The Banker" to go with it. Dad said the house had a prestigious address and would help his business.

I told him to get a life; that it's 1982 and nobody cares about "prestigious addresses," but he chose to ignore me.

When the moving van pulled up Dad asked me if I would like to go on a little walking tour of Maggie Falls while the movers were unloading. Maybe he thought that by giving me a proper introduction to town life I might like what I saw and start being a little nicer to him. (I had been giving him the silent treatment ever since he had decided to ruin my life by making me move to town with him.). I was

# The Shaman Stone

dying to get up close and personal with some of the shops lining Main Street, but I certainly wasn't going to let Dad know that, so I fixed my face into a blank mask, looked right past him as if he didn't exist, shrugged my shoulders, and said, "I don't care."

We walked along West Main past a bank, a law office, a jewelry store, and a coffee shop, as far as Dad's business, Radcliff & Sons Mortuary. We came back on the other side of West Main passing a restaurant, a clothing store, and an old-fashioned drug store with an ancient soda fountain. West Main ended at City Park where Rice Creek spills into the Indian River at Maggie Falls. Forgetting my vow of silence, I asked, "Aren't we going to cross the river to East Main?"

Dad gave a little chuckle and said, "You mean the 'low rent district?' Nothing there you want to see. Last I remember East Main was home to a tattoo parlor, pawnshop, greasy spoon diner, budget motel, and some old stores with broken windows and apartments to rent on the second floor."

We found a bench in City Park to sit on, near the plaque telling all about the Radcliffs and the other "important" people who founded the city. There is a junkyard across the river, just around the bend, down on the flats. Nobody minds it very much, however, because we can't see it from our side of the river. Upriver, beyond our old house and the Maggie Falls Cemetery, are high bluffs topped by an Indian cemetery on the west side of the river and an Indian mound on the east side.

## June Gossler Anderson

I've never actually been there but I've heard the Indian cemetery is about three hundred years old. Nobody knows how old the mound is. It's been there forever. Although it's against the law to go digging in Indian mounds, it is said they are full of the bones of Indian people who lived here a long time ago. Some people think there is buried treasure in them as well, and others say the mounds are haunted; but most people think the Indians made that story up to keep people away. A rickety old bridge connects the Indian cemetery on one side of the river to the burial mound on the opposite side. Further upriver is the Indian reservation, which is nestled between Indian River and Rice Creek. Way up north are the paper mills. We can't see .them, but we can sure smell them when the wind is right.

"Well, the furniture must be unloaded by now," said Dad. "Time for us to get back to work." As we got up to leave the park he tossed another thunderbolt. "By the way, Elizabeth Mae, I will be needing a housekeeper and someone to look after you."

"But Dad," I protested. "I am a mature thirteen and do not need a babysitter."

"I beg to differ," he said. And that's how Mrs. Keenan came into the picture.

# 2
# My Former Babysitter

Mrs. Keenan was this old biddy who thought that keeping house for Dad meant she was my keeper, too. I figured her last job must have been that of a jailer in some reform school for wayward girls. Dad never came right out and said she was my "babysitter," but she always managed to be at the house doing her housekeeping when I was home. I knew it was so she could boss me around, but Dad said she's just "keeping an eye" on me.

She must have been a hundred years old. Her face was all wrinkly and she wore her long white hair pulled back into a knot on the back of her neck. She called it a "bun." Most women, even grandmas, wear slacks unless they have to "dress up" for church or something, but not Mrs. Keenan. She wore an ugly cotton dress with a zipper up the front and ugly flowers splashed all over it. She said it was her "housedress" and that in her family only men wore the pants. She hobbled about in "sensible" black lace-up oxford shoes with her "hose" (that's what she called her stockings) rolled down into fat rings around her ankles. She complained about corns and bunions on her toes, and she smelled--not stinky; more like old people liniment that she said she needed for her "aches and pains."

Mrs. Keenan and I didn't get along very well. Being thirteen years old and going into seventh grade I didn't need someone watching me like a hawk and telling me what I can and can't do every minute of the day. I called Mrs. Keenan "Mrs. NO." "No, you can't do this. No, you can't go there. I'm responsible for you, and you might get hurt." I even had to beg and plead to be allowed to go over to Kendra's after she got back from that fancy International Language Camp where she was "immersed in the French language." (That meant she couldn't talk in English while she was there. Bummer.) Can you believe that here she is, my best friend (after Aunt Betty), and Mrs. Keenan hardly let me see her?

Mrs. Keenan took an instant dislike to my hair. I'll admit that it's long, brown and bushy, but Aunt Betty had shown me how to pull it back into a ponytail like hers so that it stayed out of my face. Mrs. Keenan told me I looked like a hippie with all that hair and that it should be short and neat. She even went so far as to make an appointment at Hackmore's Barber Shop. (Honest, that's their name, but most people refer to them as "Hack it off Barber Shop.") They specialize in "bowl cuts." That's the kind of haircut where the barber puts a bowl over your head and cuts off all the hair that straggles out from underneath it. I skipped that appointment.

Mrs. Keenan also thought I was too skinny; that I needed more "meat on my bones." So she plotted all sorts

# The Shaman Stone

of ways to "fatten me up." Now the obvious solution would be to bake cakes and make cookies if she thought I was suffering from a lack of calories, but not Mrs. Keenan. She was a health nut. No goodies in our house. She made me eat beans and peas and spinach. If it was green, that's what was on Elizabeth Mae's plate. And was she ever a fanatic about hand washing! Every time I turned around, I had to wash my hands clear up to my elbows. Germs, you know. Bossy, bossy, bossy. The only meaningful conversation we ever had was the time she informed me that my bowels should move every day. Honestly! That's what she said! Right to my face! I was so embarrassed. That's when I decided Mrs. Keenan had to go.

Now, how does one go about getting rid of a meddlesome babysitter? By being totally obnoxious, of course. Mrs. Keenan liked to listen to churchy music—hymns and such. She thought that kind of music was especially appropriate for the home of the city's mortician. I didn't agree so I tuned the radio in my room to a hard rock station, turned the volume up full blast, shut my door, and wedged a chair under the knob so she couldn't get in to turn it off. So what did Mrs. Keenan do? She turned off her hearing aid!

Then I started thinking about little creatures, particularly rodents. I had a hunch she didn't like furry little animals. Every time I brought one in the house, she'd yell, "Get that thing out of here!" Since obnoxious didn't work I decided to try a scare tactic and hatched out a plan called the "Reverse Pied Piper Plot." I bought some mice at the pet store and set them loose in the house to scare her out. It cost me two week's allowance, but I figured it would be a good investment in my sanity. So what did Mrs. Keenan do? She bought mousetraps and caught every single one. Dead! The poor creatures.

Well, she may have won that battle, but the war wasn't over yet.

One afternoon I was sitting in the backyard trying to figure out my next maneuver, when I saw the solution to my problem sunning itself on the back steps. My salvation was a big rat snake, scales glistening in the sun eager to help me rid the house of old Mrs. Keenan. Since she had successfully thwarted my two previous brainstorms I figured it was time for sheer terror. I came up with a plan so diabolical that it surprised even me.

Now I know a lot of people are afraid of snakes, but I'm not one of them. I think snakes have a certain kind of appeal. Too wiggly to be cuddly, but they make for some interesting action—completely unpredictable, which scares a lot of people.

The trick was how to catch it. Spotting a blanket hanging on the clothesline I got up very slowly, so as not to startle the sleeping snake, and inch-by-inch eased that blanket off the line. Holding the ends in both hands, I moved cautiously to the steps, and in one fell swoop, flung the blanket over the snake and wrapped the ends together, making a snake bundle. Then I brought the snake blanket

## The Shaman Stone

bundle into the house, left it on the living room floor, and went back outside.

A few minutes later, through the closed screen door, I heard Mrs. Keenan muttering, "Now how did this blanket get in here? I thought I put it out to air." Then a scream. And that's how Mrs. Keenan decided she didn't want to be our housekeeper any more.

# 3

# The Indian Grounds

With Mrs. Keenan gone, I was free to do whatever I wanted. Summer was almost over, and I had a lot of catching up to do. The day after Mrs. Keenan resigned, Kendra and I were sitting around at my house moaning about the fact that school was going to be starting and we hadn't done anything exciting together. I started to tell her about Mrs. Keenan and the snake when, all of a sudden, I got a brilliant idea. "Let's go on a picnic!"

"Dumb," said Kendra. "What's so great about a picnic?"

"We'll have this one in the cemetery. Lunch amongst the tombstones," I said in my best Bela Lugosi voice.

"Dumb again. We've been to the cemetery a dozen times, visiting all our dearly departed relatives." (I think Kendra was mocking my father when she said that "dearly departed" bit.)

She had me there. But then I had another idea, even more brilliant than the first. "Not the Maggie Falls Cemetery," I whispered, "the Indian Cemetery."

I could see I had her attention. "You mean the one on top of the bluff?"

"Right on."

Then Kendra got this holier-than-thou look on her face. "I'm not so sure we should be snooping around the Indian cemetery. They might not like it."

"Who cares?"

"Well, I have never been there before," she said rather thoughtfully.

I could tell she was warming up to the idea. One more little nudge and I knew I'd have her. "Neither have I. I hear it's haunted."

"You're kidding!"

"And I know how to get there without anybody seeing us."

The next morning, after Dad left for work, I made some sandwiches, stuffed them in a paper sack, grabbed my bike out of the garage, and met up with Kendra.

"Where's this so-called 'secret road'?" she asked.

"Follow me." We biked out to the Maggie Falls Cemetery, past Aunt Betty's house and along the river road. At the north end the dirt road kind of turns into trees, then into a forest. Leading into the thick woods were a pair of ruts overgrown with prickly bushes and baby trees. "This is an old logging road," I told Kendra. "It hasn't been used since the sawmill shut down." I could see she was impressed.

"How come you know that?" she asked.

"I used to live out here, remember?"
"Does anybody else know about this road?"
"A few old-timers. They call it 'Cemetery Road'."
"How come?"
"Now Kendra," I said imitating the tone of voice our sixth grade teacher used when he wanted us to think. "Use your head. Where are we now?"
"At the Maggie Falls Cemetery."
"And where are we going?"
"To the Indian cemetery."
"And how are we going to get there?"
"Oh, I get it! This road connects the two cemeteries."

The bike ride was harder than I had thought it would be--hot, bumpy, and lots of flies chasing us. There were some fresh tire ruts in the road, too, which we had to avoid. Kendra started complaining about my rotten idea, but I wasn't going to let on that I was beginning to agree with her, so I just said, "Shut up and keep peddling."

Finally, what was left of the old logging road disappeared and we were at the base of a bluff overlooking the Indian River. There was a big Indian mound perched on the bluff across the river. Although the river was about as wide as a four-lane highway at that point, we could hear loud, angry voices coming from the top of the mound but we couldn't make out what they were saying.

"Do you really think it's haunted?" Kendra looked worried.

# The Shaman Stone

"No." I was worried, too, but not about ghosts. Those were real people. What if they saw us? Townspeople weren't exactly welcome here.

"Let's go home," said Kendra.

"Not me. I'm hot and tired and hungry. We came here for a picnic, so let's do it."

I hid my bike in some tall grass next to the road ruts and grabbed the picnic stuff. Kendra stood next to her bike for a minute deciding what she should do. Then she hid her bike next to mine. I knew she would. Honestly, Kendra's such a chicken. If she didn't have me for a friend, she'd never have any fun.

The top of the mound across the river seemed to be occupied by the living, so Kendra and I climbed up the backside of the bluff on our side of the river where no one could see us. The brush and trees were thick and overgrown, except in a few places where there were piles of fresh dirt. When we got to the top, we found ourselves plop in the middle of the Indian cemetery.

"Look at this marker." I showed Kendra a wooden stick with a picture of an upside-down animal stuck in the ground next to a grave. Looking around, we saw lots of them-- different names, different animals, all upside-down.

A little ways away from the first graves we came upon what looked like a village of doghouses. One of them had a dish of food sitting on a mat beside the door. It looked pretty gross with ants and bugs crawling through it. We both gagged and choked for a while.

Mixed in with the burial plots were some strange diggings that sure didn't look like graves to me, and I'm somewhat of an expert on them. They were deep, round holes, not wide enough to bury anyone who's in a lying down position. I wondered if the Indians buried some of their skinnier people standing up.

We ate our lunch behind one of the little houses where we could see the people on the Indian mound across the river, but they couldn't see us. We watched them run around, bend over to pick stuff up, show it to each other, and yell some stuff we couldn't make out.

"What do you suppose they're doing?" Kendra asked

I didn't have the foggiest idea, but I wasn't going to admit that to Kendra. "Some sort of ritual dance," I said, acting like I knew what I was talking about. Then, to change the subject and take Kendra's mind off the goings-on across the river, I thought of an especially appropriate story for picnicking in a graveyard. "Do you know what a 'death watch' is?" I asked her.

"Is this going to be another one of your ghost stories?"

"Not exactly. This really happened. Lots of times. Aunt Betty told me about it."

"Okay," Kendra said with an exaggerated sigh rolling her eyes upward so they just about disappeared out of their sockets. "So what's a 'death watch'?"

# The Shaman Stone

"Well, years ago people weren't always dead when they got buried. Sometimes they were just sleeping. Really sound asleep. Or just passed out, drunk."

"You're kidding me!"

"No, honest. And do you know how people found out about this?"

"No. How?"

"Sometimes they dug up the coffins so they could use them again. And when they opened them up, they found claw marks on the lids. Like the 'dead' person woke up and was trying to get out."

"That's awful!" exclaimed Kendra.

"So after that relatives started tying a string to the dead person's finger and attaching it to a bell that was hung next to the grave. And all night long someone would have to sit by the grave to listen for the bell to ring. That was called the 'death watch.' And if the person doing death watch duty heard the 'dead ringer' ringing the bell, he'd quick grab a shovel and dig up the not-yet-dead corpse."

"You're kidding me!" Kendra looked kind of worried.

"No, it's the honest truth. So whenever you're in a cemetery and you hear a bell ringing, you better run for help, because somebody's six feet under who shouldn't be."

I had just finished telling Kendra about "death watches" and "dead ringers" when the strangest thing happened. I heard a bell ringing, softly at first, then louder and louder. And the sound was coming from somewhere within the Indian cemetery! Kendra heard it, too, and we were both scared out of our wits. Then Kendra did the dumbest thing anyone could ever do. She screamed, really loud. The people on the other side of the river stopped what they were doing and turned to look in our direction.

"Oh no! They've seen us!" Kendra shrieked. She got up and started to run. If they hadn't seen us before, they sure had now, for Kendra was right out in plain sight, running and crying like she was being chased by a herd of ghosts.

I had no choice but to leave our picnic mess behind and run after her. We tumbled down the backside of the bluff and ran through the brush until we found the place where our bikes were hidden. Kendra jumped on hers and started peddling for all she was worth. Some friend! She didn't even bother looking back to see if I was coming.

We got home from the Indian cemetery in a lot less time than it took us to get there. Our picnic was ruined. The day was ruined. And Kendra was all upset and mad at me, so she went home. When I started to think about it, I got mad, too. How was I to know that anybody else was going to be there? Our picnic was spoiled just because some Indians decided to powwow on top of an old Indian mound.

# 4
# Strangers at Maggie Falls – Trouble at Home

The last week of summer vacation was real hot. Kendra was still mad at me so I had to bribe her into going swimming at Maggie Falls by telling her she could lie in the pink satin-lined coffin in the funeral home when we got back, providing my dad was somewhere else at the time.

We like to swim in the shallow part of the river, where it hasn't been dug out by the falls, but where you can still get sprayed by the falling water. We have a special spot there on the beach where we can sit against some rocks and see everything without anybody seeing us. Usually, I see a lot of people I know, but this time there were a lot of strange (and I do mean strange) looking kids at the beach. And were they dumb! They could hardly talk English. They said a lot of funny words that I had never heard before. I think they were some kind of immigrants. Anyway, they sure didn't look like they were from these parts. My Aunt Betty says those kinds of people ought to stay in their own country. She says ours is getting too crowded with all of them moving in.

I said to Kendra, "I sure hope I don't have to go to school with any of them."

She gave me a self-righteous look and said, "We ought to keep an open mind about people we don't know."

I said, "Having an open mind is like having holes in your head for all your brains to fall out of."

Kendra's smug smile fell off her face and her jaw nearly dropped out of its socket. When she finally closed her mouth, we got into a big argument, and Kendra got so mad at me, she went home. She sure is touchy.

My summer vacation went from bad to worse. It ended when Dad came home from work, the same day Kendra and I got into our big argument at Maggie Falls. I knew I was in trouble the minute he walked in the door. His face had that tight-pinched "stay-in-control" look he always gets when he's mad about something.

"Elizabeth Mae," he said. "Come here."

I didn't argue. I didn't even stop to say, "Why?"

"Do you know what this is?" he demanded, showing me a beat-up food-stained paper bag with the name "Radcliff & Sons" printed on the side.

I was puzzled. "Yes. It's one of those bags you have printed up for people to put their sympathy cards and other junk in after a funeral."

"Do you know where I got this one?"

I had an uneasy feeling that I did.

"Sheriff Wilkins gave it to me." Dad was talking louder and louder. He was beginning to lose it. "The sheriff

# The Shaman Stone

brought it into my office and asked if I knew anything about it." He paused before continuing. "And do you know where he got it?"

"From the trash?" I asked hopefully.

"No! From the Indian cemetery! Somebody was up there having a picnic!"

"Who?" I asked innocently, trying to stay in the game.

"Two girls. While he was there checking out some complaints of vandalism, the sheriff saw two girls."

"Does he know who they were?" I tried to seem genuinely interested.

"The question is do *you* know who they were?" I could feel his eyes probing into my brain as he asked the sixty-four dollar question. "Elizabeth Mae, where did you go on your bike ride last Tuesday?"

I knew the game was up. The rules were I could use strategy to evade Dad's questions, but never lie outright. "To the Indian cemetery," I admitted. "But gee, Dad, we were only having a little fun. I don't know what's so wrong about that."

"Elizabeth Mae," he said sternly. "Those burial grounds are sacred to the Indians. We don't allow people to play in our cemetery out of respect for our dead. And you have no business playing in theirs. I would think that being the undertaker's daughter you would have more sense than to pull such a stupid trick. But apparently you don't." Taking a deep breath, he delivered the final blow. "Since I can't trust you to use good judgment, you're grounded until further notice."

"But Dad…" I wailed.

"And furthermore, you are never to go out to the Indian grounds without permission."

The next night Aunt Betty came over to talk with Dad about hiring someone to keep an eye on me and keep house for him. I tried to convince them that I was too old for a babysitter. Dad said, "I was beginning to think maybe you *were* old enough to take care of yourself, but after that stunt you pulled at the Indian cemetery, I don't think so."

"But Dad…" I moaned. "I'm almost thirteen."

Then Aunt Betty's eyes lit up so bright I could almost see a neon sign flashing above her head saying, "Idea! Brilliant idea! Hear me out!"

"Elizabeth Mae, don't argue with your father," she said, winking at me. "I know just the person to stay with you. She's lots of fun. Wanda will be great."

"Wanda who? Great for what?"

"Wiley's wife, Wanda. She'll be a perfect nanny. Besides, Wiley's not working right now and they need the money."

"Nanny!" I wailed. "I don't need a nanny!"

"Now Elizabeth Mae, settle down," said my dad. I could see the look of relief on his face. Then he turned to Aunt Betty. "Didn't you graduate from high school with Wiley?"

"Not exactly. We went to school together, but Wiley never graduated. Said he didn't know what good all that learning was going to do him. Said all he wanted to do was be a truck driver, and he didn't need to know all that other junk to drive a truck. So he dropped out of school and his father bought him a dump truck for an 'ungraduation' present."

"If he's got his own truck, how come he's not working?" Dad asked.

"Uh," Aunt Betty said, obviously looking for the right words. "It seems he ran into a bit of bad luck, and now nobody will hire him." She continued in a rush of words. "So, you see, they really need the money. And I just know Wanda will make a wonderful nanny for Elizabeth Mae and keep an immaculate house for you."

Dad doesn't always agree with Aunt Betty, but he usually gives in to her on household matters. So now I have a nanny, Wanda the Wonderful. She starts the first day of school.

# 5
# Not So Wonderful Wanda

Besides being the first day of school, yesterday had to be the worst day of my life, both at school and at home. First of all, one of those foreigners I saw at Maggie Falls when Kendra and I had our big fight is in my language arts class. He's weird looking, with dark skin, straight black hair and slanty, slitty eyes. His name is Vue and he's from Laos--wherever that is. He doesn't speak any English and Ms Oiler says we should be nice to him and try to help him because he's been through a lot--whatever that means.

One of the Indian boys from the reservation north of town is in my language arts class, too. His name is Heron, but he reminds me more of a hawk. His eyes look like they can see right through you. He's never been in a town school before, because he's always gone to school on the reservation.

Kendra's in my math class, but since that day at Maggie Falls, we're not friends anymore. She says I'm "prejudiced" and she doesn't want to hang around with "prejudiced people."

## The Shaman Stone

I said, "Fine. Be that way, but don't ask me to help you with math when you get stuck on division of fractions."

When I got home from my perfectly terrible day at school, I was greeted at the door by my new nanny, Wonderful Wanda. She was wearing black spandex pants and a low cut, black tank top that barely covered her boobs. Her black eyes were underlined with massive amounts of eyeliner, and her long oily black hair hung halfway down her backside. I've seen pictures of some movie stars dressed that way. I think it's supposed to be sexy or something. But Wanda looked plain scary.

Curling her blood red lips over a mouthful of rotten teeth, she smiled the most sinister smile I've ever seen and hissed, "It's about time you got home. Now get in here and get this place picked up."

I looked inside. Dirty dishes and candy wrappers were everywhere. "Wait a minute," I protested. "*I* didn't make this mess. Besides, this is *your* job. *You* pick it up. That's what *you're* getting paid for."

"Wrong," she snarled. "I was hired to be your nanny. You mind *me* or I'll take care of *you*. Get my drift? Now get going."

The nasty look on her unpleasant face told me I better not fool around with her. I picked up her sticky wrappers and washed the dishes while Wanda the Wonderful made herself comfortable on the sofa watching a TV soap and drinking a can of diet pop to wash down the chocolate covered cherries she was slurping on.

During the commercial she disappeared into the kitchen. I heard the refrigerator door open and close, and then the beep of the microwave. She had timed it perfectly, returning to her soap just as the commercial faded.

"Supper's on the table," she announced, plopping herself on the sofa again. "And make sure you clean up after yourself."

I went into the kitchen and there on the table wrapped in paper toweling was a nuked hot dog in a bun with a half-eaten box of potato chips sitting next to it. I got some ketchup out of the refrigerator, poured myself a glass of milk, and feasted in solitary. Dad had to work late, so I was in bed when he came home. Wanda had already left.

In the morning before Dad went to work, I tried to talk to him about Wanda, but he wouldn't listen; just said something about behaving myself, minding her, and not getting into trouble.

"But Dad," I wailed. "She makes me do *all* the work!"

"It's about time you started helping out around the house," he said. "I'm afraid Mrs. Keenan has spoiled you."

Maybe I'll have to take matters into my own hands, like I did with Mrs. Keenan. Problem is Wanda's too mean to be scared of snakes. They're probably afraid of her.

# 6
# Meet Mr. Herrington

With Wanda the Wonderful reigning as Queen of the Radcliff Household, I was in no hurry to go home after school so I stopped by the drugstore on Fourth and Main to see how the remodeling was coming along. Some guy from New York bought it from Old Man Larson. Good thing, too. My dad says Old Man Larson was getting so old and senile that you never knew what he was putting in your prescription. Dad thinks that some of Old Man Larson's customers ended up being customers of Radcliff & Sons-- prematurely.

Every carpenter and plumber in town was busy working on the soda fountain. They said the new owner had it shipped out from New York. The sign above the store said "d' Angelo's Pharmacy and Soda Shop." A cute boy (if you like boys) was busy sweeping out the place. I think he's the new owner's son.

I started to go home, and then decided to ride my bike out to Aunt Betty's instead. I wanted to talk to her about not-so-Wonderful Wanda. Now that she and dad have split the business Aunt Betty takes care of the cemetery. She sees that the grass is mowed and graves are dug, and sells cemetery plots when somebody dies.

The Radcliff burying ground is right next to the cemetery. It has a cave dug into the hillside with a door in it. My dad calls it a "crypt." The first Radcliffs were buried there. After a while, it got too crowded, so they began burying the rest of the Radcliffs in plots at the bottom of the hill. You can't see the crypt from the house but you can see the gravestones inside the big wrought iron fence surrounding them from my bedroom window. Sometimes Aunt Betty and I visit the family plot where my mother is buried along with my grandparents and the rest of the Radcliffs, "resting for eternity." Those are my father's words again. I'll probably rest there someday, too, except I won't be a Radcliff if I decide to get married.

Aunt Betty had company. He must have been pretty important because she was wearing a skirt and blouse instead of her usual jeans and t-shirt, and had twisted her ponytail into a fancy French knot, wearing it the way she did for her Founding Families meetings. "Elizabeth Mae," she said in her "let's impress the company" voice. "I would like you to meet Mr. Fred Herrington." From the way she bustled around getting me a root beer I figured Mr. Herrington was some sort of celebrity. "Mr. Herrington has come to look at the grave sites. He's also very interested in old cemeteries…and," she added, "He's an author. He writes books about old pioneer families, like ours, for a big book publisher in Minneapolis."

# The Shaman Stone

Aunt Betty's big round kitchen table was a mess, as usual, full of her genealogical papers that she's always working on. She's really into family history. I think she's trying to link us up to the Mayflower. I pushed a pile of papers out of the way to make room for my pop can. Then I moved a stack of books and papers from a chair so I could sit down.

Mr. Herrington was a rather small man, not much taller than Aunt Betty, but even though he wasn't big he had a lot of muscles. His dark hair was cut short and it looked like someone had drawn a moustache over his upper lip with an eyebrow pencil. The rest of his face was shaved clean and he smelled of cologne. Unlike most of the men in Maggie Falls, who either wear business suits or blue jeans, he had on khaki pants and a short-sleeved plaid button-down shirt. Only one thing seemed out of place. His hands were rough with traces of dirt stuck in the cracks of his skin and underneath his broken fingernails.

Mr. Herrington was all right. At least he talked to me like I was a real person, not like Aunt Betty's shaggy-haired boyfriends who either ignored me or said dumb things like, "And how old are you?" because they can't think of anything intelligent to say to a "little child."

I didn't have a chance to say anything to Aunt Betty about Wanda since Mr. Herrington was there. I finished up my root beer and went home to my wonderful nanny who made me wipe up the kitchen floor that she had spilled pop all over as punishment for my being late.

# 7

# Stone Sickness

The day after I met Mr. Herrington at Aunt Betty's I biked back to her house after school. I still needed to talk to her about Wanda. I figured that since Aunt Betty had gotten her hired, she should get her fired. That witch was becoming hazardous to my health, and Dad wouldn't even listen to me.

I was almost to Aunt Betty's house when I saw something really strange lying in the middle of the path. It was a rock about the size and shape of a small egg, but flatter and bluish colored. It looked like it had been tumbled smooth in Maggie Falls for a long time. But when my foot turned it over, I could see there was something very different about it. It had markings on it; some kind of pictures carved right into it, and it glowed. I'm not kidding. There was a light shining from it. Well, maybe it was just reflecting the sunlight. It was definitely not the kind of object you leave on the path right in plain sight for just anybody to steal. So I picked it up and put it in my backpack for safekeeping.

# The Shaman Stone

Aunt Betty wasn't home. I intended to leave and go back to town but all of a sudden I found myself in the cemetery next to my mother's grave, and I was holding that strange stone with the funny pictures carved on it right there in my hand! I could have sworn I had put it in my backpack! What on earth was that stone doing back in my hand and how did I end up inside that plot? The black wrought-iron fence surrounding the graves was standing tall and the gate was closed. I don't remember either opening or closing that gate, much less walking though it. Did that rock have anything to do with it, or was I losing my mind, or both?

I was still wondering how I managed to end up in the Radcliff plot when I heard the tinkling of a bell, a small bell that seemed to get larger as the ringing became louder. It was like the bell we heard at the Indian cemetery when Kendra got so scared. I had an awful thought: What if someone had been buried alive out here and was ringing the bell for help!

Then, I don't know whether I should have been scared or happy, because I saw my mother! I knew it was my mother because I always carry a picture of her in a heart-shaped golden locket Dad had given me when I was a little baby. "This way," he had told me, "your mother will always be close to you--next to your heart."

Mother was reaching out her hand like she wanted me to take hold of it. I almost did, but then I thought, *What if she drags me back down into the grave with her?* I got so scared that I ran out through the gate, made a beeline for my bike, and pedaled as fast as I could all the way home. Then I felt kind of bad because I thought maybe she had wanted to tell me something. I didn't say anything to Dad about it, because he'd think I was nuts. And it might make him feel bad, too. I think he still misses my mother.

Luckily, Wanda was on the phone when I got home, so she didn't notice me come in. I fixed myself a bologna sandwich and went up to my room. I tried to do some homework but I couldn't concentrate. My mind kept racing and thoughts kept crowding to the surface. I tried to tell myself that it hadn't really happened. Dad says there's no such things as ghosts even though he is an undertaker and has a close relationship with the dead. Maybe I had been wide-awake and dreaming, if that's possible. And then there is the matter of that rock...

I was feeling kind of odd--maybe it was the bologna sandwich I hadn't finished eating--so I went to bed. At least that's what I thought I did. Next thing I knew, I was in the Indian cemetery holding that rock in my hand. Both of my feet were stuck in some mud and I had a hard time moving. I think I was what you might call a "captive audience."

The Indians weren't there this time, but the bell was—ringing in my head. Were the dead people buried here coming for me, too? Instead of being scared, a really weird feeling came over me, like part of me was very young and part of me was very old. Then I saw them—blue lights dancing on top of the mound across the river from me. At first I thought it was lightning, except the flashes

## The Shaman Stone

were coming out of the mound and shooting into the sky instead of the other way around. I wanted to run but my legs wouldn't work. I had to stay and watch those lights weaving in and out in some sort of a ghost dance. The bell was getting louder and I was getting scared.

All of a sudden, the stone jumped out of my hand and bopped me on the ear! That's all I remember 'cause next thing I knew I was lying in my bed. I thought maybe I had had a bad dream, but my ear was bleeding and my muddy shoes were still on my feet getting the bed covers all dirty.

I didn't feel very well when I got up the next day. Dad took one look at me and insisted I go to the doctor. Wouldn't you know it, though, Dr. Hanson was meeting with some doctors at the Mayo Clinic down in Rochester and that new black doctor from one of those cannibal islands way out in the middle of the ocean that Aunt Betty had warned me about, was on duty.

I told Dad I didn't want to see no witch doctor who would probably cast a voodoo spell on me and then tell me to call him in the morning--if I wasn't dead. Dad told me to stop being ridiculous and to mind my manners.

The doctor looked at my ear and shined a flashlight in my eyes. He said I had a small concussion and that I should rest in bed for a few days. He asked me how I had hurt my ear. I was tempted to tell him that Wanda had hit me, but I didn't. I didn't dare tell him what had really happened because he'd either think I was crazy or I'd get in trouble for going to the Indian grounds without permission. So I muttered something about falling and hitting my head against the end of my bed.

    I got a lot of rest. The only one who came to see me the first day I was home sick was Wanda the Witch who had to be there because she was being paid to babysit me. Wanda might have been an awful nanny, but she was a worse nurse. She crabbed at me all morning about the mud on my bedspread, but didn't bother to change it. She poured me a bowl of dry cereal for breakfast. I had to get the milk and a spoon myself. Then she sat in the living room to watch her soaps and talk on the phone.

    My head hurt and I felt dizzy. I lay in bed trying to rest. I even managed to doze off for a while until the smell of cigarette smoke woke me up. That really made me mad. Cigarettes were absolutely forbidden in our house, and here was Nurse Nanny puffing away on the weed right in our very own living room! I'd never wished more for a bedroom phone than I did right then. I needed to call my dad and get her fired. But I didn't dare risk the wrath of Wanda by using the kitchen phone. She would probably see me or hear me. I was getting dizzy just thinking about it. Feeling miserable, I fell asleep again.

    Things got worse. I was awakened by a man's voice that I had never heard before coming from the living room. I picked up the rock hoping it would spirit me away again, but it didn't. I got out of bed very quietly and crawled on my hands and knees to my bedroom door, pushing it open a

# The Shaman Stone

crack so I could look down into the living room. There, on the sofa, I saw Wanda and some creepy looking guy puffing away and drinking beer. He must have been her husband, Wiley. Judging from the pile of beer cans littering the living room, they must have been partying for quite a while.

Well, coming from one who has seen a ghost, this scene was far more scary. If Wiley was half as nasty as his wife, Wanda, I could be in real trouble. As softly as I could, I closed my bedroom door and put a chair under the doorknob. I didn't know if it would do any good, but that's the way they do it in the movies. I figured that if they decided to come in my room, at least the chair under the doorknob trick would give me time to jump out of my second story window. My head was really hurting now.

I must have dozed off again, for the next thing I knew, I was awakened by more loud voices, and one of them was my father's. Through the closed bedroom door I heard him yell, "Get out of here! Both of you!" Then the sweetest words of all, "You're fired!"

Wanda started screaming. "That's the thanks I get for taking care of your miserable little brat!"

And Wiley was yelling, "You can't fire her! Breach of contract! We'll sue!"

Then the front door slammed, and all was quiet.

Dad came up and tried my bedroom door. It wouldn't open. I scrambled out of bed and moved the chair.

"You all right?" he asked.

"I guess so."

"Your Aunt Betty's a good woman, but she's a lousy judge of character."

*So are you,* I thought. But I kept it to myself. I could see he was pretty upset.

# 8

# A Desperate Situation

The doctor told Dad I had to stay in bed and "take it easy" for a few days which was probably a good idea since every time I got up my head started hurting. But even so, I was bored and lonesome. Nobody from school came to see me, not even my one-time friend, Kendra.

Aunt Betty and Mr. Herrington came on Saturday, but they didn't bother talking to me. They sat there in my bedroom and yakked about the book Mr. Herrington says he's researching in Maggie Falls. Something about the descendants of the early Colonists and the cities they founded as they moved westward from the Colonies. That really hit Aunt Betty's hot button with her being descended from the Radcliffs and being as she is president of the Maggie Falls Chapter of Founding Families.

Aunt Betty was so enraptured with what Mr. Herrington had to say that she paid absolutely no attention to me. You'd think that after all I'd been through she would have shown a little more concern for her favorite (and only) niece.

Her friend, Mr. Herrington, was more enraptured by the stone on my dresser than he was in visiting with me. I caught him staring at it every chance he got. When Dad came in my bedroom to ask Aunt Betty about some business thing, Mr. Herrington got up out of his chair pretending to look out of the window next to my dresser, but he didn't fool me. He just wanted a closer look at that rock. I actually saw his hand move towards it, like he was going to stuff it into his pocket, but when he looked around to see if anyone was watching, he saw that I was. He nodded in a stupid sort of way and pretended to look out the window some more. When Dad left, he sat down again, just like nothing had happened, and yakked with Aunt Betty some more.

Honestly, I don't know why I don't just throw that darn rock out the window. My life is complicated enough without that crazy thing glowing at me all hours of the night. I even thought of giving it to Mr. Herrington since he seemed to be so interested in it, but a voice inside my head told me not to.

Dad waited on me hand and foot all day Sunday. "Can I get you this? Can I get you that? How are you feeling? Are you hungry?" He never came right out and said it, but I could tell by the way he was acting that he was sorry he hadn't listened to me when I tried to tell him about Wanda. I knew he was getting a little worried, too, with it being Sunday and him having to go back to work on Monday.

# The Shaman Stone

I overheard him talking on the phone with Aunt Betty. He was trying to get her to come stay with me until I was well enough to go back to school, but she said she was much too busy introducing Mr. Herrington to her friends, "the descendants of the town's founding fathers, whom he'll be interviewing for his upcoming book." I felt kind of bad. Aunt Betty used to love to sit with me.

In the evening I came downstairs to keep Dad company and watch the ten o'clock news with him. I still wasn't feeling very good. He had called all over town trying to get someone to stay with me so he could go to work on Monday.

"I have a problem," he admitted. "Where am I going to get someone to keep an eye on you until the doctor says you can go back to school?"

Since he wasn't having much luck I figured this might be a good time to bring up the subject of "Why I Am Too Old to Need a Babysitter Anymore."

"Dad," I said in my most mature voice. "You know I'm thirteen. Most thirteen-year-old kids don't need babysitters."

"Elizabeth Mae" he said, "Most thirteen year-old kids show better judgment than to trespass on Indian burial grounds."

So I made a mistake. And he wasn't ever going to let me forget it. Well, two can play that game. I was really getting mad. "And most fathers of thirteen year-old kids have better judgment than to hire someone like Wanda to look after their kids."

Almost as soon as I said it, I wished I hadn't. I had thought he'd just get mad at me and we'd argue some more, but instead he blinked a few times and said in a soft voice, "You're right. I made an awful mistake hiring Wanda. I should have checked her out myself. I just thought it would be nice for you to have someone to come home to instead of an empty house." Then he added, "Maybe *you* don't need someone to look after *you* anymore, but *I* need someone to keep the house up for us while I work, unless you want to take on that responsibility."

I'd never looked at it from that angle before. I sure didn't want to be in charge of the housework. "Well Dad," I said, "how about a compromise?"

"Like what?"

"*You* hire someone to look after the house and let *me* look after Elizabeth Mae."

"Do you think you can keep Elizabeth Mae from getting into trouble?"

I looked at Dad in surprise. I couldn't believe he'd give up this easy. He hadn't. I said "Of course I can," and he said "You're going to have to show me first," and we were right back where we started from—except he couldn't find anyone to look after the house, or me.

The sports news was almost over when the doorbell rang. Dad answered it. There, standing on the doorstep was an Indian woman. She was older than my dad, but not as old as I remembered my grandma being before she passed. She wore a brightly colored long dress with a full skirt and moccasins. Beaded earrings dangled from her ears and two

## The Shaman Stone

long black braids with strands of gray hair woven through them draped over her shoulders and slid down her back.

"My name is Annie Birdsong," she said. "I understand you need a housekeeper."

# 9

# The New Nanny

Annie Birdsong reported for work bright and early the next morning. Dad let her in before he left. When I woke up I could hear her moving around downstairs. It sounded like she was doing something in the kitchen. Then I heard her feet on the stair treads, moving slowly and deliberately as if she were trying to sneak upstairs without waking me. Well, I'd fool her. I sat up in bed waiting for the door to open. Instead, I heard a soft knock and a voice say, "May I come in?" I guess I was the one who was surprised. Neither Mrs. Keenan nor Wanda had ever thought of knocking and asking permission. They'd just barge right in whenever they felt like it. I didn't know what this new housekeeper was up to, so I figured I'd better let her know right from the start, sick or not, that she'd better not mess around with me.

"Come in," I said.

Annie Birdsong pushed the door open and walked over to my bed. She looked the same as she did the night before, except this morning she was carrying a big tray with some interesting looking things on it.

# The Shaman Stone

"I'm not hungry," I said, hoping she couldn't hear my stomach growling, "and my head hurts. Get it out of here."

She smiled and said, "I'll just leave the tray here and you can eat some when you feel like it." And she left.

I tried my best to ignore it, but she had baked a muffin. It was hot out of the oven. Blueberry. How could she have known that was my favorite? Then I checked the teapot wondering what was in it because I didn't see any teabag strings hanging over the side. I sniffed it. It smelled spicy and earthy all at the same time. I tried a sip. It tasted good and first thing I knew I had eaten the muffin and drunk the tea and was feeling wonderfully drowsy.

I woke up from my nap when Annie Birdsong knocked on my door. "How are you feeling?"

My headache was gone, but I wasn't going to let on to her that I was feeling any better. "So, so," I said.

She smiled a strange little smile. I think she knew her tea had done its trick.

# 10
## Aunt Betty's Visit

That night there was a big fight when Aunt Betty came over. First of all she was upset about the foreigners moving into town. "They're a disgrace to Maggie Falls," she complained. "They live in the worst part of town. It's so run-down that decent folks moved out of there years ago. It's nothing but a slum, the Maggie Falls Slums!"

"Maybe that's all they can afford," Dad suggested.

Aunt Betty continued to rant and rave. "Soon they'll be taking over the whole town. And when that happens, that'll be the end of Maggie Falls!"

"According to who?" Dad asked.

"According to Mr. Herrington. And he ought to know. Says he's seen it happen often enough. Those foreigners move in and decent people move out, and that's the end of towns like Maggie Falls. They're ruined!"

Dad looked pained, but he knew better than to argue with Aunt Betty when she was on a rampage. "Do you have time for a cup of coffee?" While he was filling her mug he said, "Don't mean to change the subject, but how are things with the FF?"

# The Shaman Stone

Her expression lightened up and she beamed, "Couldn't be better. I've introduced Mr. Herrington to about half the members of the Founding Families and next week he's going to speak at our meeting."

Dad looked puzzled.

"He's writing a book about the Founding Families," she explained. "And I am to be his editorial assistant. Our family will be in the book and my name will be on the cover, along with Mr. Herrington's." She looked very pleased with herself.

Then Aunt Betty changed the subject and turned to me. "Sorry that Wanda didn't work out, Hon. I thought you'd like her." Then she asked Dad, "Are you going to be able to get another housekeeper?"

"Matter of fact, I already have."

"Oh? Who?" Aunt Betty looked happy for Dad and relieved for herself.

"A woman by the name of Annie Birdsong."

"Birdsong?" snapped Aunt Betty, the smile falling from her face. "From the reservation?"

"Well, not exactly. She's staying in town until the big powwow."

"She's Indian!" Aunt Betty spat the words out.

"Appears to be."

"Who referred her?" Aunt Betty demanded.

"Guess she kind of referred herself."

"No references?" Aunt Betty was really getting hot.

"Didn't even think to ask." She just appeared on my doorstep. Like the answer to a prayer."

"Oh brother!" shouted Aunt Betty. "How can you be so stupid? You've got to be careful around those Indians. They'll steal you blind!"

Now Dad was starting to get angry. "What about 'Wonderful Wanda'!" he yelled. "Did you bother to check *her* references? Did you even *know* the woman before you told me to hire her?"

Aunt Betty slowly got up from her chair and drew herself proudly and stiffly to her full five feet two inches. "Wanda was recommended by her mother-in-law who just happens to be Wiley's mother and one of our most prominent FF members," she hissed. "Mrs. Quackenbush is the descendent of one of Maggie Falls' founding fathers."

"And the mother of one of its worst citizens," added my dad.

The argument was over because Aunt Betty walked out of the house, slamming the door behind her.

# 11

# Annie Birdsong

Annie Birdsong came again the next morning. I heard her downstairs talking to Dad. Then the door closed. I wondered if it was Dad or Annie who was leaving, but soon I heard her foot on the stairs and a knock on my door. I was really confused. I didn't know how I should act towards her. Aunt Betty was so against her being here. It made my head throb just thinking about it.

"Good morning," she said as she pushed the door open. "I have your breakfast." She gave me a quizzical look. "Your head hurting again?"

"Yes," I said forgetting about how I should act towards her.

Annie Birdsong laid her hand on my forehead, just like Aunt Betty used to do when she wanted to see if I had a temperature. Almost instantly the throbbing stopped and my brain seemed to stretch out and relax. My head felt so good.

"Your dad had a headache, too. I fixed him some tea before he left for work and he felt better."

Annie straightened up my room while I ate the blueberry muffin and drank the tea she had made for me. When she rearranged the items on my dresser, she did a rather strange thing. She took the carved stone out of my open dresser drawer where I had dumped it with my other junk and set it very carefully in a special spot she had cleared off on my dresser. Then she spoke to it very softly and in words I didn't understand. I know she didn't think I could hear her because she looked startled when I asked, "What did you say?"

She quickly smiled again. "Oh, I said to come downstairs for a while and keep me company if you feel up to it." She picked up my breakfast tray and left the room.

By lunchtime I was feeling better, much better, so I went downstairs to eat. Annie had fixed a hotdish. She said it was a wild rice casserole and that I should try some. I poked around in it for a while, but I couldn't find anything green in it—no peas, beans, or spinach or stuff like that which Mrs. Keenan used to hide in her hot dishes. It actually tasted good. When I asked Annie what it was, she just answered, "Old Indian recipe."

Annie sat across from me at the kitchen table while I ate. She had two baskets made out of birch bark. One of them contained what looked like can lids. She curled one of the lids around a cone-shaped piece of wood forming it into a miniature ice cream cone, flattened the end with a pair of pliers, and plopped it into the other basket.

"What are you doing?" I asked.

# The Shaman Stone

"Making jingles," she replied.

"What for?"

"My dress. I'm a Jingle Dress Dancer."

"What's a Jingle Dress Dance?"

"It's a special dance we do at powwows. I'm a champion Jingle Dress Dancer," she said matter-of-factly.

"Are you going to be dancing at a powwow?"

"Yes."

"When?"

"After the wild-ricing. All the local tribes are getting together for a big intertribal powwow in Grand Portage. I must dance again if I am to remain the champion."

Wild-ricing. I knew that the Indians on the reservation pack up lock, stock and barrel around the end of September to go wild ricing. I couldn't explain it, but all of a sudden I felt kind of panicky as I asked Annie Birdsong my next question. "Will you be coming back to keep house for us after the powwow?"

She looked very thoughtful and said, "When my work here is done, I'll return to my home."

"What work? This housekeeping job?"

"No," she smiled. "More important than that."

"Is Jingle Dancing your work?"

"No," she said.

I couldn't think of any more questions to ask her.

# 12

# A Meeting of KWWKers

Dad came home early yesterday to take me to the doctor. Luckily Dr. Hanson was back so I didn't have to see the witch doctor from the cannibal island. The doctor looked at the side of my head where the rock had smashed me, shined a flashlight in my eyes, and asked me how I felt. "I think she can go back to school tomorrow," he told Dad.

So there I was, back in school. That voodoo doctor's daughter, her name is René, is in my class. I heard she and her father are from some dirt-poor island in the Caribbean that everybody's trying to get out of. Kendra seems to like her, now that we're not friends anymore, probably because both their fathers are doctors at the clinic. They even have their own secret language. Well, I couldn't care less. I'm not talking to her anymore. I just give her dirty looks. I overheard Kendra tell someone that I was giving her the "evil eye" and that she's going to join some kind of "quack" club. Big deal.

Some other kids showed up in class while I was gone. More foreigners. Ms Oiler says they're Hmong. (She pronounces it "mung" to rhyme with "hung.") I think they're the ones Aunt Betty was saying had moved into the Maggie Falls slums across the river.

I can't believe what happened! I stuck around after school the day of the first KWWK (pronounced "Quack") meeting. I didn't have a clue what it was all about, probably because the information went out while I was stuck in bed and nobody bothered to tell me anything about it. But I figured that if it was good enough for that stuck-up Kendra and her new friend, it was good enough for me, so I went just to see what was going on. I was surprised to see a lot of kids from my seventh grade class and the eighth grade class there. They probably didn't have anything better to do.

The Indian boy, Heron, who is in my language arts class, was there, too. Nobody was paying much attention to me so I sat at a table pretending to read a book. But I was really eavesdropping on Heron. He was talking to another boy about some stuff going on at the reservation.

"We had to call the sheriff in to investigate," the one called Heron was telling the other boy. That's when my ears perked up. "The burial grounds were a mess. Somebody had gotten hold of a posthole digger and made holes all over the place. They even punched through some of the graves and dug up the bones in the old cemetery. Left them scattered all over the ground. The elders were furious!"

"That's understandable," said the other boy. "Our elders would be mad, too."

I was surprised to hear him say that. His back was to me but obviously he was a foreigner--people in Maggie Falls don't call old people "elders"-- but you couldn't tell it by the way he talked.

"So somebody was digging up the old cemetery," repeated the boy. "When did this happen?"

"As close as they can figure," said Heron, "during the summer. The shaman is very worried about it. He's afraid the old legend will come true."

"What legend is that?"

*"When bone and stone see the sun, the work of the evil one is done."*

I was practically falling off my chair trying to hear the rest of the story when Ms Sutton, the KWWK coordinator, called the meeting to order. I figured I was at the wrong place when she explained that KWWK stands for "Kids Working With Kids." That meant if someone is having a problem he or she will be able to turn to a person of his or her own age for help.

I don't know why I stuck around for this. I thought this was going to be a fun group. If someone is having a problem, that's *their* problem. Actually, what I really wanted to hear was the rest of Heron's story.

Ms Sutton said, "There are a lot of new kids in school whose biggest problem right now is that they can't talk to anyone here because they can't speak English."

# The Shaman Stone

*Maybe they should go back to their own country where they can speak their own language,* I thought.

"What they need most is a one-on-one relationship with someone who will help them learn to speak English and be their friend." Then she looked right at me. "Elizabeth Mae, I have a very important assignment for you. There is a special person in this school who, I think, you would be able to help immensely. Would you come to my office after school tomorrow to meet him, please?"

Well, I couldn't exactly say 'no' with all those kids looking at me. I think I just got roped in to becoming a "quacker." I wonder who the "special student" I'm supposed to help is?

I biked out to Aunt Betty's before going home to tell her about the vandalism in the Indian cemetery and my new KWWKer job. Mr. Herrington was there again. "Well," he said, "I'm not surprised that someone is digging in those graves." He turned and faced me, eyeball to eyeball. "You know what they're looking for?"

I said I didn't have the foggiest idea.

"Bones," he hissed. "Indian bones."

"What on earth do they want bones for?" Aunt Betty asked.

"Medicine."

"Huh?" I said. "Medicine? For who?"

"Well," he said. "You're a smart little cookie. Let's see if you can put two and two together. There's a lot of

Asians around, aren't there?" (Except he didn't say Asians.)

"What's that got to do with the Indian cemetery?" I asked.

"Everybody knows about the ingredients for their 'special medicine'," he said.

*Special medicine?* I didn't know what he was getting at.

"You should know," said Mr. Herrington, "that they grind up the old Indian bones and drink it in their tea. They think it gives them special powers."

I couldn't believe it. I thought of Vue, the Hmong boy in my class. Even though he was weird looking, he didn't look like a tea-bone juice drinker to me. In fact, I think Mr. Herrington was just making it up to impress Aunt Betty with how smart he was.

"And who do you suppose is grinding up all those Indian bones and selling them for medicine?" Mr. Herrington asked.

"Who?" said Aunt Betty leaning forward, all ears, her eyes nearly popping out of her head.

"That new pharmacist. The one who just moved here from New York with his fancy soda fountain. That's just a front, you know. He's making big money dealing in the Indian bones black market."

"Really!" exclaimed Aunt Betty. "With all these foreigners and New York gangsters moving in, Maggie Falls is going to become the crime capital of the state!" She was really getting upset. "There ought to be a law against them!"

Mr. Herrington flashed a know-it-all smile at Aunt Betty and winked at me. I didn't return his smile. Even though I wasn't friends with any of the Hmong kids in school, he didn't have to mean-mouth their families. And I knew he was lying through his teeth about d'Angelo's drugstore, but how could I make Aunt Betty believe me?

# 13

# Jingle Bells

I was surprised to see Annie still hanging around the house when I got home from Aunt Betty's. Now that I'm back in school and totally responsible for my behavior I don't need anyone telling me what to do and checking me in and out of the house. I half expected Annie to chew me out because I was late, but instead she had supper in the oven, and a blueberry muffin sitting alongside a glass of milk for me. She sat across the table while I ate, making jingles. At first neither of us said anything. I ate the muffin and Annie curled the lids into cones.

"How many of those do you have to make?" I asked breaking the silence.

"Three hundred sixty-five. One for each day of the year."

"That's a lot. Why don't you just go out and buy some bells?"

"That's not the Indian way. Wanna help?"

"I don't know how."

"I'll show you." Annie demonstrated how to roll the pliable snuff can lids into miniature ice cream cones,

## The Shaman Stone

pinching the tops over short cloth strips with a pair of pliers. While we rolled jingles, she told me about the powwow she was preparing the dress for. "There are a lot of powwows all over the country every weekend. I can't go to them all, but I am going to go to the big intertribal one this fall. Tribes from all over the United States will be there."

"Just what is a powwow?" I had heard of powwows but I had no idea what they were all about.

Annie reached for another snuff can lid and rolled it around in her fingers for a minute before she spoke. "They are a big gathering. Indians come from many tribes to sing and dance and gamble, and visit with friends and family. But most of all, powwows are a celebration. They make us feel happy."

"Does everyone dance in the Jingle Dress competition?"

"Almost everyone dances but there are many dance categories besides Jingle Dress Dancing."

"Like what?"

"Oh," she said. "There is the Men's and Woman's Traditional Dance, the Fancy Dance, Grass Dance--lots of dances."

"Both men and women dance?"

"Yes, but not at the same time," she laughed.

"You don't dance with each other?"

"No. We dance in a big circle. Each dance is different. The Jingle Dress Dance is special because it was first used by our people for healing."

"Are you a healer?" I asked remembering her touch on my forehead that took away my headache.

Annie Birdsong looked past me, out the window into space, "I am," she replied softly. She didn't say anything more for a long time. I tried to think of another topic of conversation. "Do you know a boy named Heron?"

"Yes," said Annie. "He's in your class at the school this year, isn't he?"

*How did she know that?* "Yes. I think he's new to the school."

"That's because he went to the Indian school on the reservation. Now his father thinks he needs to go to school in town." Annie took a long strip of cloth and sewed the tape of one of the bells to it.

"I overheard him talking to another one of the new kids," I said, "about the diggings at the Indian burial grounds." Then I stopped. *Did Annie Birdsong know about them?* I asked her if she did.

"Yes," she said. "It makes me very sad to know that someone is disturbing sacred Indian bones."

"Heron said something rather strange," I told her. "It was about bones and stones and evil. He said it was an old legend, but I don't remember how it went."

"Sounds like an old Indian story. About the shaman."

"What are shamans?"

"Shamans are special people, our spiritual leaders. Some of them can communicate with the spirit world. Many of them are healers."

# The Shaman Stone

I looked at Annie for a minute. I thought of her healing powers and her strange ability to know what I was thinking. "Can shamans be women?" I asked.

"Yes."

"Are you a shaman?"

"Yes--and more." Annie's face didn't change expression, but her eyes clouded over with faraway thoughts and her voice seemed to speak from the depths of a long time ago. We sat for a few more minutes without talking. To break the silence I looked at Annie's birch bark basket full of jingles and laughed.

"What's so funny?" she said coming back into herself.

"Dad doesn't allow tobacco in the house and just look in your basket. If someone saw all those snuff can lids they'd think we were freaking out on nicotine."

Annie laughed then said, "Nicotine is the white man's curse, but tobacco is sacred to the Indian."

# 14

# Special Assignment

I stopped by Ms Suttons's office after school to see who my "special assignment" was. I just about dropped my teeth. It was Vue! Thinking fast I said, "I'm sorry Ms Sutton, I've changed my mind. My dad needs me to help around the house, so I won't have time to be a KWWKer."

"I'm so sorry to hear that," said Ms Sutton. "I know Vue will be disappointed."

"He will?" I couldn't imagine anyone being disappointed that I wouldn't be around.

"Yes. He asked for you to be his special helper."

"Asked for me? How could he? He doesn't even speak English."

"The interpreter showed him the yearbook pictures of your last year's class and asked him to choose the person he wanted to work with him. He pointed to you."

"He did?" I looked at Vue standing over by the blackboard. He looked more helpless than weird. He smiled a little smile then pointed to me and then to himself and nodded "yes" as if it were a question. Well, maybe he

# The Shaman Stone

wasn't as weird looking as I thought. I found myself nodding "yes" back at him.

I think I heard Ms Sutton heave a sigh of relief as she motioned for us both to sit at the table.

"I'm not saying I'll be a KWWKer," I said, "but if I am, just what am I supposed to do?"

"Talk to Vue."

"Talk to him? I thought that was the problem! He can't understand my talk. It's English."

"That's just the point. He needs to hear someone talking English--just to him-- so he can become familiar with the sounds of our language."

"What about the meaning of those sounds?" I asked. "I'm going to feel like a complete idiot babbling on and on to someone who doesn't understand a word I'm saying."

"Then it's up to you to help him understand what those sounds mean."

"And just how do I do that?"

Ms Sutton reached for a pile of little kids' pictures books. "It's a lot like reading to your little brother or sister."

"I don't have a little brother or sister. I'm an only child."

"No problem. Read the pictures. Point to a picture and say its name. Then have Vue repeat the name back to you."

"Is that all?"

"No. You need to think of lots of ways to get your ideas across so he can understand you," she explained.

"How?"
"One way is to act it out."
"I'm no actress," I said. "I'd feel stupid."
"You've already had a good start.
"Being stupid?"
"No," said Ms Sutton. "Acting it out."
"Huh?"
"How did you say 'yes' to him?"
"I smiled and nodded my head."
"So, you're an actress."
"And you want me to be an English teacher, too," I said. "I'm going to have to think about this."

Annie had a muffin and milk waiting for me on the table when I got home.
While I ate she worked on her jingle dress. Finally she looked up. "Is something bothering you?"
I was still trying to sort out my feelings about Vue and I wasn't ready to share them with anyone so I said, "It's my hair. It's always such a mess." Since Aunt Betty and I had parted ways, my hair seemed to have taken on a life of its own.
"You want some help with it"
"What kind of help?"
"Let's try braiding it." Annie ran a comb through my hair and almost magically the snarls untangled and it lay smooth and flat, ready for braiding. As she plaited the strands into a single braid down my back she said, "Now, what else is bothering you?"

# The Shaman Stone

I figured I might as well share my thoughts with her. She always seemed to know what I was thinking, anyway. "Well," I said. "We have a lot of foreigners in school and I'm not so sure they belong in Maggie Falls."

"Why not?" Annie tied off the braid.

"Aunt Betty and Mr. Herrington say they'll ruin the town."

"How's that?"

"They live in the Maggie Falls Slums and can't even speak English. Aunt Betty says they should be sent back to where they came from." I didn't tell her what Mr. Herrington had said about their drinking Indian bone tea.

"And where's that?" asked Annie.

"Some country on the other side of the world. I think it's in Asia,"

"Do you agree with Aunt Betty?"

"I don't know," I replied. "Anyway, I've been asked to help one of the boys learn English."

"Are you going to do it?"

"I don't know. Aunt Betty says we shouldn't have anything to do with foreigners. They're different."

"We were all foreigners once," stated Annie.

"Not me," I told her. "I was born right here in Maggie Falls."

"But your people were foreigners. They were born someplace else."

"My people?"

"Your ancestors."

"They came over from Europe. But that was a long time ago."

"But they *were* foreigners," insisted Annie Birdsong giving my new braid a tug.

"Well, *we* were here first!" I could be just as stubborn.

"Not exactly," said Annie. "I seem to remember something about Pilgrims inviting Indians to a Thanksgiving Dinner."

I had to give her that point.

"Even my people were foreigners once," continued Annie. "Many years ago, the world was much colder than it is now. Much of the earth's water was locked up in ice and some parts of today's oceans were actually dry ground."

"That was called the 'Ice Age,' wasn't it?"

"You're right," said Annie. "Huge sheets of ice covered North America all the way to southern Minnesota and the Iowa border. The Bering Sea between Siberia and Alaska wasn't water then, but a great expanse of dry ground. It was called a 'land bridge' even though it was several hundred miles wide north to south."

"So, what's that got to do with your ancestors?"

"Back in the Beginning of Time, my ancestors lived in the far eastern part of Siberia, but over a period of many hundreds of years, they followed the big game animals that they hunted across the land bridge into what is now Alaska. Then, as the ice melted, they fanned out all over North and South America. Even though that happened thousands of years ago, they *were* 'foreigners' at one time."

## The Shaman Stone

"I guess they were," I agreed. Then it struck me. "Siberia! That's in Asia, isn't it?"

# 15

# A Conflict of Interests

I've got a problem—big time. It started with Vue and ended with Aunt Betty. The first KWWKer session was scheduled to be held after school yesterday. I had pretty much decided to forget about it. After all, if Vue's people drink Indian bone tea like Mr. Herrington said, (even though he was probably lying) I figured it would be better to have nothing to do with him. Aunt Betty always says, "You're known by the company you keep," and "Better safe than sorry." Then I got a notice from Ms Sutton. It was more like an invitation, inviting all the KWWKers to meet at the soda fountain in d'Angelo's Drug Store after our sessions for a chocolate soda, compliments of KWWK. That was too good an offer to pass up.

After school I checked out some easy books from the library making sure they had plenty of pictures. Vue and I got together in a corner of the library and I pointed to the pictures and said the naming word. He gave me a funny look, so I pointed to his chest and said, "You." Then I pointed to my mouth and said, "Say word."

# The Shaman Stone

I guess he got the general idea because he started repeating the words after me. "Ball, house, baby, car..." Then we came to the picture of an airplane. Vue got real excited. He put his arms out like wings and started flying around the room saying "airplane...new home...America!" He flew over to the globe and spun it to the other side of the world. He pointed to a country somewhere in Asia saying, "Old home. No good."

I looked at where he was pointing. The name on the globe said "Laos." I guess he didn't like it there. Then we started acting out some phrases like "Open the door." "Shut the door." "Stamp your foot." "Hit the table." "Put the chair on the table." "Stick out your tongue." We were finding a lot of zany things to do, but it was getting harder to do them because we were so busy laughing.

The librarian came over and told us we were too noisy and would have to leave. That was okay with us because it was almost four o'clock; time to meet the rest of the KWWKers at the drugstore for a soda.

D'Angelo's Pharmacy was starting to look like a little United Nations. All it needed was some flags. Kendra and René were sitting by themselves in a big booth. The rest of the booths were filled with a lot of kids I didn't know. I also didn't know where we were going to sit until Kendra patted the seat next to her and said, "Sit with us," just as if we were still friends. I think the cold war was beginning to thaw.

She and René were giggling. I introduced them to Vue as best I could. "I'm helping him with his English," I explained.

"I'm supposed to be helping René with her English, too," said Kendra, "Except she doesn't need any help. So she's teaching me French."

"French?" I said. "I thought you were from some island in the Caribbean."

"Oui, Mademoiselle," said René with an exaggerated French accent. "On ze Island of Haiti, we speak ze French."

We all burst out laughing, even Vue, who, I am sure, didn't understand a word of what was going on.

" René s going to be living here for two years while her father completes his medical residency," Kendra said.

"He's a doctor," added René .

"I know," I said. "We've met. Where's your father going after he finishes his residency?"

"Back to Haiti."

"I thought people wanted to *leave* Haiti," I said remembering a newspaper article we had just discussed in class. "What on earth does he want to go back for?"

"Heal people. Save lives," she said jokingly. But the look in her eyes told me she was serious.

Ms Sutton walked in with Heron and one of the Hmong boys. Everybody cheered wildly. After all, she was paying the bill. The boys looked for an empty table and saw that there was still room at ours. "Can we sit here?" asked Heron. We all moved over to make room for them.

# The Shaman Stone

Tony d'Angelo, son of the new owner, came over to take our orders—all chocolate sodas. We goofed around for a while and blew straw wrappers at each other. Then Kendra asked Heron, "What's you friend's name."

"Pao," said Heron.

I thought I would try out my newly acquired English teaching skills on him. "Where house?" I asked outlining the shape of a house with my arms. Pao looked at me with a puzzled expression. No good. I'd try again. "Where you live?" I said pointing to him on the word "you." Again, a blank look.

I was just about to try again when Pao turned to Heron and said, "Doesn't she speak English?"

Then I recognized his voice. He was the boy Heron had been talking to at the KWWK orientation. I felt pretty foolish, but everybody else thought it was pretty funny. I had to laugh, too.

"In answer to your question," said Pao. "I live with my parents on a farm on the river bottoms just outside of town. We raise vegetables. Next spring we'll be opening a greenhouse to raise specialty crops for Hmong cooking."

Ms Sutton announced that since we were all together, we were going to have an informal meeting. "Pao has something he wants to discuss with us." She nodded to Pao. "The floor is all yours."

Pao stood up so we could all see him and talked loud enough so we could all hear him. "Fellow KWWKers," he began. We laughed and started quacking like ducks until Ms. Sutton shushed us. "The Hmongtown

Hmong are planning a little celebration to celebrate the harvest and they have invited the whole town of Maggie Falls to be their guests."

"What's it going to be like?" asked a voice.

"Oh, the usual," replied Pao. "Hmong singing, Hmong dancing, Hmong cooking-- and a soccer tournament." Everybody cheered. When we quieted down, he continued. "The elders thought it would be a good idea and they asked if the KWWKers could get it organized and sign up the teams."

There was a lot of discussion but everyone liked the idea. Ms Sutton said it would be good for our group to have a project. We discussed the make-up of the teams and decided on open membership. That meant that our teams would be made up of both Hmong players and anyone else who wished to play. Some of the more artsy KWWKers said they would make posters advertising for members and some of the more persuasive KWWKers said they would begin signing up players.

I was feeling pretty good about myself and about the KWWKers when I left the drugstore. I just had to share those feelings with someone so I biked over to see Aunt Betty.

For once she was home and not running all over town with Mr. Herrington. I babbled on and on about Vue, and Pao, and Kendra, and René, and the soccer tournament. Then I noticed the expression on her face. Obviously, she didn't share my sentiments.

"Elizabeth Mae," she said sternly. "I don't like the idea of you hanging around with those foreigners. They're not like us. They're not American."

"Of course they're not," I said with all the lightheartedness I could muster. " René is from Haiti. Vue is from Laos…."

"Laos?" interrupted Aunt Betty. "That's in Asia, isn't it? Aren't they the people who make tea out of Indian bones? Fred – er – Mr. Herrington says their favorite food is dog meat."

"Mr. Herrington says this, and Mr. Herrington says that…" Aunt Betty was relentless as she went on and on about why I shouldn't associate with "those people." That happy feeling I had brought to share with her dissolved into numbness. I felt torn between two worlds. *Those people* were my new friends, but Aunt Betty had always been my best friend.

# 16
## Lost Souls

I haven't seen much of Aunt Betty since the first KWWK session. I think she's mad at me, and I don't feel very comfortable around her. I miss the old Aunt Betty, the one who was my best friend before Mr. Herrington came into the picture. Dad says she's got a one-track mind; that when she's on a roll she can't think of anything else. It happened when she took a research-writing course in college and decided she would research Maggie Falls. She spent a whole year digging in libraries and talking to all the old people in town, and jabbering on and on about all her "wonderful discoveries" at breakfast, lunch, and dinner. Dad said she was "obsessing." But, even though she monopolized the conversation, all that research was a good thing in her life, and a real boon to the city when she got *The History of Maggie Falls* published as a book. But she's changed since she's been hanging out with Mr. Herrington. He seems to have cast a spell over her. I think he's cast a spell over most of the town, as well.

# The Shaman Stone

Kendra told me that Mr. Herrington had stopped over at her house to interview her mother for his book. Some of Kendra's ancestors came to Minnesota territory with my many times great-grandfather, Henry Radcliff.

"Mr. Herrington told my mother he had signed a contract with a big publisher in New York who was going to pay him a lot of money for the book," Kendra said. "Mr. Herrington also told her that he was going to donate the profits to the Founding Families Association here in Maggie Falls. Mom was really excited about meeting a 'real author' who wanted to include our family in his book," Kendra continued "She went on and on talking about all her dearly departed family members while Mr. Herrington sat there holding a long yellow pad of paper and a pen. It was kind of odd, though. He hardly wrote anything down on that paper, just made a few doodles." She thought a moment. "Maybe he's got a good memory."

I told her that Mr. Herrington has asked Aunt Betty to be his "editorial assistant." "He spends a lot of time at her house and she seems to be pretty impressed with him. Everything he says she takes as the gospel truth. Personally, I think he's pretty disgusting, especially the way he talks about people he doesn't even know."

"I agree," said Kendra. "I really got mad when he started bad-mouthing those 'Asian foreigners who are ruining the town.' He was telling Mom something about 'bone tea,' but I couldn't hear it all because I had to study for my French quiz."

"He's already met with a lot of Founding Family members," I said. "I wonder who else he's been telling about Indian bone tea."

Then I had a strange thought. *Hadn't Mr. Herrington told Aunt Betty the book publisher was in Minneapolis?*

Vue is catching on to English really fast. Of course I can't take all the credit for his success. He has special help at school and the aunt and uncle he lives with talk English to him all the time. Ms Oiler says his aunt was a translator for American relief workers in the refugee camp in Thailand, so she knows a lot of words. Vue is past the picture book stage of learning now, so mostly we spend our KWWK time gabbing with the help of Pao who interprets both ways when the going gets tough.

Today Vue told us a real hairy story about how he got to the New World. He said that when his flight landed in Chicago, he thought he was in Maggie Falls, so he got off the plane to look for his aunt and uncle. Actually, he was supposed to transfer to a commuter plane. They're the only ones that can land at the Maggie Falls airport because it's so small. But nobody bothered to tell him that. Or if they did, he didn't understand them.

"I look all over airport for Auntie and Uncle," he said. "Not there. I look outside airport building for them. Not there, either. I walk around for a while and pretty soon airport building not there either. I'm lost. It's getting dark out. I'm getting cold and I'm hungry. I stop man to ask for

# The Shaman Stone

help, but I can't make him understand. Then, two people on corner start fighting with each other. Sirens. Police come. I run away."

"Weren't you scared?"

"No, things worse in Laos. Police catch you there, you gone."

"Gone? Where?"

Vue shrugged his shoulders. "Who knows? Jail. Prison. Maybe worse..."

"Then what did you do?"

"I walk around all night. Listen to people yelling. Guns shooting. Finally I find doorway. Curl up. Go to sleep."

"Were you scared then?"

"Not until men in uniform come. Shine big light in my face. They got guns and sticks for hitting people."

"Did they hit you?"

"No, silly," Vue laughed. "This America, not Laos. They put me in squad car and talk on car phone. Take me to stationhouse. And guess what?"

"What?"

"Auntie waiting for me there. She crying."

And I thought the Pilgrims had it tough.

# 17
# In The Beginning

Today all my teachers piled on the homework. I almost broke my back lugging the books home. As soon as I walked in the door I cleared off a spot on the dining room table and set to work conjugating verbs, reading about the American Revolution, and trying to decide which side of the equation "x" belonged on.

After a while I had a feeling that I wasn't alone. Someone or something was watching me. I looked around to see if Annie was there, but she must have been running an errand. Then I saw the stone shimmering on my desk. I was sure I had left it on my dresser. I picked it up to put it back where it belonged when--Bang!--I wasn't in the dining room anymore. I was standing at the bottom of the bluffs overlooking the Indian River. But, everything was different! For one thing, there was snow on the ground-- little splotches here and there. Snow in September? No way! The trees were weird, too. Their leaves were small and bright green, like they were just budding out. Impossible! Last I remember it was almost fall. Leaves are supposed to be turning red and yellow and orange and

# The Shaman Stone

dropping to the ground. And the plants along the base of the bluff weren't brown and dying; they were green and growing. Somehow, it was spring! And, strangest of all, even though it was a clear day, I couldn't see the old bridge that connected both sides of the river north of the mounds. It had disappeared!

I knew it wasn't warm out because I could see my breath. I wasn't wearing a coat, but I wasn't cold. Although I thought I knew where I was, it was entirely different. The air smelled fresh--no stink from the paper mills--the river water looked clean enough to drink--no crud floating downstream--and the bluffs didn't seem nearly as high as I knew them to be.

In the distance I saw a bunch of canoes heading downstream towards me. As they came nearer I could see they weren't the aluminum rental variety. In fact, the closer they got, the less they looked like canoes and the more they looked like big floating logs--with strange furry-looking critters in them using fat sticks to paddle them down the river. At first I thought the log creatures might be some little Big Foots, you know like Yeti or Abominable Snowman, but as they got closer I saw that they were more like shaggy-haired human beings wearing skins and furs for clothes. I didn't know if I should hide or not before they saw me. After all, I wasn't supposed to be here! I decided to stay put. There wasn't any place to hide anyways.

When they got to the riverbank I could see that the logs they were riding in were hollowed out, like the dugout canoes I had seen in a *National Geographic Magazine*. The hairy people beached their logs where I was standing, but didn't pay any attention to me. It was as if they couldn't see me. They were shouting and making strange sounds, like they were trying to talk to each other, but their words, if that's what they were, didn't make any sense to me. (They must have been foreigners.) Don't ask me how, but even though I didn't understand their words, I knew what they were saying and I understood what they were doing. Their first order of business was to unload the log canoes. They must have been planning to stay for a long time because it looked like they were carrying all their junk with them.

Men, women and children got busy emptying the canoes and setting up camp. Some of the men went into the woods and returned with tall skinny trees they must have just cut down because the ends were sharp and dripping sap. I wondered how they had managed to chop them down because I didn't see an axe or a hatchet anywhere, not even a knife. Some of the men stuck the poles in the ground in a large circle then started hanging skins over them to make some kind of a wigwam.

Several of the women got busy picking up driftwood from the beach and the little kids added some dry brush to the woodpile. It looked like they were going to try to make a fire, but they must have forgotten their matches because they were hitting some stones together over dry grass, like Boy Scouts. To my surprise, they soon had a roaring fire going. I was even more surprised to see some of the kids carrying fist-sized rocks up from the riverbank and dropping them into the fire. I expected some of the

# The Shaman Stone

grown-ups to start yelling at them to "stop playing with the fire," but nobody seemed to care.

While the fire blazed away the people unloaded pots and baskets from the log canoes and brought them over by the fire. They hooked the baskets on long sticks that were set in the crotches of two V-shaped sticks stuck in the ground next to the fire pit, and started filling them with water from the river. I was impressed. The baskets hardly leaked at all.

When the stones the kids had thrown into the fire got hot, some of the braver ones scooped them out of the flames with some flat bone-like objects and dropped them into the hanging baskets. Were they cooking rocks, or boiling water? I decided they must have been boiling water because after awhile I could see steam rising out of the baskets. They took what looked like dried bits of meat from the clay pots and dropped them into the hot water and some of the women added some stuff that looked like roots, probably vegetables of some sort that I had seen them digging out of the ground. Then I realized they weren't cooking rocks. It looked like they were making soup!

While the food cooked I snooped around the camp. I thought maybe I was like a ghost because nobody seemed to be able to see me. Either that or they were doing a very good job of ignoring me. However, there was one old woman who seemed to know I was there. Her face looked like it was made of leather. It was furrowed with wrinkles, and her long hair was mostly gray. Unlike the others, she wore a beaded skin pouch around her neck. She glanced in my direction from time to time and nodded as if she knew me. Somehow, it seemed as if I should know her, too.

After the wigwams were built and the soup eaten, I sat on a rock and watched the people take the last of the bundles out of the canoes. They were lumpy looking packages; some wrapped in skins, some in furs, some even in birch bark. Several people picked up the bundles while the rest of the group filled their now empty baskets and pots with dirt they dug out of the ground using shovels that looked like they had been made from the bones of some very large animals. (They might have been dinosaur bones, but I wasn't sure if there had ever been dinosaurs in Minnesota.) Then, with the old woman in the lead, they got into a long line and wound their way up to the top of the bluff. She beckoned for me to follow.

Something was very wrong! The bluff was there, but the Indian mound that was supposed to be on top was missing! It didn't look like it had been bulldozed because the ground wasn't messed up; no fresh scars in the earth or piles of dirt on top. It was as if the mound had never existed! The people climbing the hill didn't seem to notice that anything was wrong so I tucked that mystery away in a corner of my brain to think about later.

Once on top of the bluff the people carrying the pots and baskets made a big circle while the old woman told the bundle bearers what to do. Using their bone shovels some of the men stepped forward and dug shallow holes in the ground, one for each of the bundles. Then the men with the bundles stuck them in the depressions and some more people stepped out of the circle and laid stone tools and little statues and clay cooking pots in the holes with them and went back to the circle.

When the old woman started to chant I felt as if I were in some sort of a church. Her voice rose to the heavens and, as if it had been summoned, an eagle flew from the tall pine on the other side of the river over the group of people. As if that were the signal she had been waiting for, the woman placed a handful of dirt on top of each of the bundles. That was the cue for the rest of the people to do the same. Carrying their pots and baskets they circled the wrapped bundles throwing dirt on each one until the containers were empty and the bundles were covered, making a small mound of dirt on top of the bluff.

I think I had just witnessed a funeral.

I thought it would be a nice touch to put some flowers on the graves, myself, so I picked a bunch of dandelions growing under some nearby trees. I had barely begun decorating the mound when—whoosh—I was back at my study table hanging on to some droopy dandelions.

Annie walked in the door just about that time with a sackful of groceries for supper. While she fixed our meal, I told her about my strange experience. I knew I could trust her not to laugh at me or tell me I needed to have my head examined.

"Those were the Ancient Ones," she said putting the casserole in the oven. "They were the first people to live on this land. Every spring they would come back to their gathering place along the river to fish for sturgeon during the summer and gather wild rice in the fall."

"Sturgeon? I didn't know we had sturgeon in this river."

"Used to."

"Aren't they humungous fish?"

"Can get up to two hundred pounds. Feed a village for a week."

"What village?" I demanded. "And what happened to the mound?"

"Those villages are long gone. But the mound is here."

"What was in those bundles that they buried?"

"Bones," Annie replied. "They were the bones of our ancestors who had died during the winter. Their bodies were placed on high scaffolds for safekeeping. Then on the return trip to the Spring Gathering Place, the people gathered up the bones and bundled them in furs and birch bark so they could be buried in the sacred mound."

"But the mound wasn't there yet," I protested.

"That was the beginning." Annie looked at the stone shimmering on my desk next to the wilted dandelions. She picked it up and held it for a moment. "This is a very special stone," she said handing it to me. "Keep it close. It will protect you from the evil ones."

"Well, it hasn't done a very good job so far," I said putting the stone back on my desk. "It almost put me in the hospital."

# The Shaman Stone

"There was a reason." Annie reached into her pocket. "I have something for you." She gave me a small leather pouch, decorated with beautiful beadwork. "This is very old. It is made from the skin of an otter. Put the stone in here and keep it with you."

I picked the stone up, put it in the otter skin pouch, and pulled the long drawstring closed.

"Let me help you," said Annie taking the pouch. "Slip the drawstring around your neck and wear it next to your body."

"What makes this stone so special?"

"It's a powerful amulet. It is the Shaman Stone."

As she slipped the drawstring over my neck, I realized something was very wrong.

"Oh, Annie," I cried. "I've lost my mother's locket!"

# 18

# A Chance Encounter

Today was HOT. In fact it was so hot they dismissed school early. All the kids seemed to have something to do that didn't include me, so I wandered out to Maggie Falls. There's a spot there that's so private no one can see you unless they really look. Sometimes I like to go out there just to think. Today was one of those days. First, I thought about the last time I had been to Maggie Falls. It had been with Kendra when we had our big fight over who's prejudiced and who's not. And then I started thinking about bones and ancient funerals.

I was getting really involved with my thoughts when I realized company was coming. It was Mr. Herrington. I probably should have said "Hello," or something, just to be polite, but I didn't feel like talking to anyone, especially him, so I slouched down behind some rocks so he couldn't see me. I was glad I didn't show myself because who do you suppose turned up right after Mr. Herrington? Wanda's creepy husband, Wiley Quackenbush. I didn't even know they knew each other, but then I figured maybe Mr. Herrington was going to interview him for his book. It's hard to believe Wiley belongs to one of the old pioneer families. His ancestors have probably rolled over in their graves and disowned him.

Mr. Herrington offered Wiley a beer and they sat down to talk. I hadn't planned to spy on them, but I wasn't about to get up to leave and let them know I had seen them together. Mr. Herrington and Wiley talked and drank for a long time. I wasn't actually eavesdropping on their conversation for the more beer they drank the louder their voices became.

The first voice I heard was that of Mr. Herrington: "Yeah, Wiley. I've got to hand it to you. You sure do know the right people around here. That was pure genius on your part, introducing me to Betty Radcliff. She's a good connection and her place is perfect for our little project."

Then Wiley's voice said, "Me and her was schoolmates. She let me dig graves out at the cemetery to make some money after the cops took my driver's license and I couldn't hire out my dump truck anymore. So I returned the favor and introduced her to you." He made kind of a snorting noise at the "introduced" part.

"Well, legal or not, you're driving your truck now, aren't you Wiley?" said the voice of Mr. Herrington with an evil laugh at the end.

"Yep, and I'm getting even with those 'better-than-you' Radcliffs for firing Wanda."

"I think we can finish up our little project pretty quick now," said Mr. Herrington. "The Indians will all be out of the way for awhile. They've gone up the creek to go wild-ricing for the week. So I'm going to take care of business and make life uncomfortable for some recent immigrants at the same time."

"You mean those Hmong people?"

"The very ones."

"Whatta you got against them?"

"They're from Asia. I despise Asians."

"Asia's a long ways away. What did they ever do to you?"

"Cheated me out of my life's work, that's what they did," said Mr. Herrington, his voice getting loud and angry. "I was well on my way to being an archaeologist, and a darn good one. Almost had an internship from the university in the bag to go on a big dig with some of the top guns in the field when this gook came along and beat me out of it. I ran out of cash to finish college and that was the end of my promising career."

"Gooks?" said Wiley. "What are 'gooks'?"

"Koreans, you idiot!" shouted Mr. Herrington. "They're Koreans!"

"Korea? That's in Asia, ain't it?"

Peeking through a space between two boulders, I saw Mr. Herrington stand up and kick the empty beer cans, making them scatter all over the beach. "So now I mine the mounds for 'gold'," he said as he and Wiley left arm in arm holding each other up.

# The Shaman Stone

I hunkered back down behind the big rock that had hidden me from their view. Now I had something else to worry about. How was Wiley going to get even with us Radcliffs? How was Mr. Herrington going to "make life uncomfortable" for the Hmong immigrants? And now he calls himself a gold miner? I thought he was a book writer.

# 19

# A Deadly Epidemic

The KWWKers met after school the next day. Even though it had cooled off a bit, the air was hot and muggy. Heron wasn't with the group. He had been excused from school for the week to go wild-ricing. Up to this point he had been quite faithful about attending our KWWK gatherings. He and Pao hung out a lot together and co-chaired the committee to organize the soccer tournament for the Hmong Festival. Pao gave the soccer report. He said it was looking good and that he and Heron had enough kids signed up for a round robin. There would be three games with six teams playing. The team with the most wins would be the winner. In case of a tie, the team with the most goals scored would win. It sounded good to the rest of us KWWKers.

Pao squeezed into the booth with Kendra, René, Vue, and me. Then he and Vue lapsed into their own language. Their facial expressions told us they were discussing something very serious.

"Hey you guys," said Kendra. "Talk English." It was an unwritten rule that when you were with the

# The Shaman Stone

KWWKers, you spoke a language everyone could understand.

"Sorry," said Pao. "We were talking about our Granny Shaman. She's worried about something and has been warning our people about an evil spirit. My mother says it's a 'premonition'."

"What's a 'Granny Shaman'?" asked Kendra.

"She's an old grandma and a shaman," said Pao. "She lives in Hmongtown."

"A shaman!" exclaimed Kendra. "Isn't that like a witch doctor? Does she practice Voodoo?"

René shot Kendra a dirty look, but only I saw it.

"No," said Pao. "She's a healer. When a person becomes sick, their spirit leaves their body. The shaman must go look for the spirit and call it back. She calls upon the spirits of her ancestors to help her."

"What about evil spirits?" I asked.

"She brings a sword with to protect her from them," Pao said. "The last time she visited the spirits, they warned her about an evil spirit here that means harm for our people."

"Do you really believe that stuff?" asked Kendra.

"Yes," said Pao and Vue in unison.

Pao's explanation of Granny Shaman's premonition bothered me a lot. I could sense an evil presence also, but it didn't reside in the spirit world. I thought of the Shaman Stone that resided on my dresser top in the otter skin bag Annie had given me. When I got home I took the bag containing the amulet from my dresser and hung it around my neck, as Annie had advised me to do. *Better safe than sorry,* Aunt Betty always said. I also felt the need for protection.

That night thunder rumbled in accompaniment to the sheet lightning generated by the heat of the day. It flashed in the northern sky and I found myself paying another visit to the spirit world. I arrived not at the Indian mound this time, but in the Indian village across the river. I knew I was not in my time, but in a time past. The air was thick with sadness. I saw a familiar figure going from tepee to tepee and heard a great wailing from within. I recognized the Indian woman from "the beginning of time," the one who had led the funeral rites on the burial mound, and realized that she was also a healer, a shaman. But, what was she doing here?

Again, as before, the shaman was the only one who seemed to know I was there, and I had a premonition that we would meet again in a future life. Like a shadow I followed her from tepee to tepee. Sick men, women, and little kids lay around the hearth fires, their faces covered with perspiration and their skin covered with angry red spots. I watched the shaman give them herbs and call to the spirits of the ancestors to help her people. She took a small tubular shaped stone out of her amulet bag. Placing it over the sores of her patient she sucked on it to draw the evil spirit from the sick one's body. But the shaman's medicine was not powerful enough to heal this strange sickness.

## The Shaman Stone

One by one the sick ones died. The shaman placed the sucking stones in their hands, wrapping their fingers around them. Then the sad procession began-- the survivors ferrying their dead across the river in canoes to the burial ground on the bluff. I stayed close to the shaman hoping to learn from her what was going on. She didn't speak to me in words, but rather in thoughts.

I recognized the cemetery as the one Kendra and I had picnicked on in another time. Small houses dotting the burying ground offered shelter to the spirits of the dead as they wandered the earth for a year and a day before crossing over. This time there would be no spirit houses to offer comfort to the souls of the newly dead or worldly goods to accompany them on their journey. There were too many bodies and too few survivors to tend to their needs. The men took the iron bladed shovels they had brought with them and started to dig holes in the earth for graves while the women lamented the deaths of their little ones and children cried for their parents. A few tokens of their lives on earth were buried with each body.

After the burials, those villagers who had survived the spotted sickness held a council. In their grief, they blamed the shaman for the deaths of the people. They said her medicine was no good; that she was possessed by an evil spirit. They decided that the only way to rid the village of the evil that was killing all the people was to kill the shaman. Since the sucking stones were no longer curing her patients, the tribal council decided to appease the spirits by stoning the healer.

She accepted her death sentence bravely, standing calmly for as long as she could as rock after rock slammed into her body. I watched with horror until it was over; then went to the dying shaman knowing no one could see me but her. As I cradled her bloodied head in my lap in an attempt to comfort her, she whispered her last words, *"When bone and stone see the sun, the work of the Evil One is done."*

I woke up in my own bed in my own time feeling overwhelmed by a great sadness. A light rain pattered against my window. The heat wave had been broken. When I didn't appear for breakfast, Annie came upstairs to check on me. She asked me what was wrong.

"I had a bad dream."

"Do you want to tell me about it?"

I said "yes" although I had a feeling that she already knew what it was about.

"In my dream," I began, "I visited the Indian village. Not the one that's there today, but one from long ago. Everywhere, people were dying from the 'spotted sickness' and the shaman healer couldn't help them."

"Those were sad times," Annie said. "Our people remember it well. The spotted sickness was a gift from the white man called 'measles'."

"Measles? I had the measles. That's a childhood disease. Nobody dies from the measles!"

"Indians did. It was a new sickness for them that their bodies could not understand and could not fight."

"You mean they had no immunity to it."

# The Shaman Stone

"Exactly. Even the shamans were powerless to conquer that evil," Annie said. "Their medicine was not powerful enough." Then she added, "The white man did give the Indians one useful gift, however."

"What was that?"

"Iron shovels. To bury their dead."

The specter of the dead and the stoning of the shaman were becoming too much for me. "Oh, Annie," I cried. "I used to be a normal person. Why are these things happening to me?"

"Maybe the Stone is trying to show you something," she replied softly.

# 20

# A Visit with Aunt Mai

Vue and I still get together for our "English" session, although our KWWKers group seems to be falling apart. Some of the kids who were paired up with the Hmong kids aren't coming to the meetings anymore and seem to have lost interest in being friends. And some of the kids who never even got to know them are saying some really rotten stuff about them. Poor Ms Sutton feels terrible about the whole situation. It's been hard to recruit teams for the soccer tournament, too. A lot of kids have dropped out and we've only been able to come up with enough players to field two teams, so I guess it will be a one game tournament instead of a three game round robin.

    After our last session Vue invited me to his house to meet his aunt. They live in "Hmongtown," the old part of Maggie Falls across the river where the buildings are pretty ramshackle and dilapidated. I hadn't been there for quite a while and going there now was like traveling to another country.

    Some of the old buildings had been torn down, but most of them had been fixed up and painted, housing little

# The Shaman Stone

shops and stores on the ground levels. Vue took me into one of the shops. "I live here," he said.

In the front was a long high counter for waiting on people, separating it from the back of the shop where a woman was hard at work at a sewing machine. Next to her machine were racks of suits and dresses, and on the walls hung quilt-like hangings with colorful pictures embroidered on them.

"You live here?" I said to Vue.

"Yes, yes, my house."

"Where's you bed?"

"In bedroom," he said and burst out laughing. "Upstairs in apartment."

I felt kind of stupid, not realizing until then that most of the shopkeepers in that mostly Hmong community lived in rooms above their shops.

Vue introduced me to his Aunt Mai. She was a very pleasant person with a face that could have been any age. "I'm very happy to meet you," she said bowing low. "You have been a good friend to Vue. You have helped him very much learn to become a real American like you."

I knew Vue's aunt meant every word of the praise she was heaping on me, but even so, I felt embarrassed. I was glad Vue couldn't understand most of it.

I decided to return the compliment. "Vue is a very good student. He tries hard and learns fast." I almost added, "And he's lots of fun," but I didn't want his aunt to think he wasn't taking his studies seriously.

"Yes, yes. You very good teacher." Aunt Mai took a deep breath. I was afraid it was to continue singing my praises, so I decided to change the subject fast.

"Are you really Vue's aunt?" *Of course she is*, I thought after the words were out of my mouth. *What a dumb question.* So I followed it up with another question that was probably none of my business. "Where are his mother and father?"

Aunt Mai's eyes started to mist over, and then I really felt bad. "I'm sorry," I said. "I shouldn't be poking my nose into your business. Maybe I should go now."

"No, no. It's all right. You stay. Have cup of tea." She lit the burner of a little gas plate that was sitting on a table and set a teakettle full of water on to boil. "Sit," she said motioning to a chair next to the table. "I will tell you about Vue."

"Vue's father, who was my sister's husband, was a warrior," she began. "Like many men of our village he was recruited by the Americans to fight the Pathet Lao guerillas. They promised to protect the Hmong people whose lives would be in danger if the U.S. left Laos. Vue's father was killed in a place called the 'Plain of Jars.' Soon after, the guerillas took control and the American soldiers had to leave in a hurry."

The tea water had started to boil, and Aunt Mai paused to pour some of it into my cup. "When the Americans left, our villagers, along with many other Hmong villagers, had to flee through the jungles and across the Mekong River to refugee camps in Thailand to escape

# The Shaman Stone

the Pathet Lao soldiers who wanted to kill us. We left everything we owned behind. But Thailand did not want us. 'Too many people,' they said. 'Too many mouths to feed'."

"How awful! Where did you go?"

"Back to Laos," Mai said. "They put us on buses and sent us back. Our family had gotten separated. Vue was with his mother on the first bus. He was just a little boy then, about the age of my little sister. I was on the fourth bus with my mother and father and my sister and brother. The buses went as far as the border. When we arrived it was night. The border guards made us get out of the buses and we were forced to pick our way down a narrow mountain trail back into Laos. The Pathet Lao soldiers had booby-trapped the trail and many, especially those on the first bus, were killed. I found out much later that Vue had escaped the fate that most surely befell his mother.

"Because we had helped the Americans, the soldiers were hunting us down like animals. We had to hide in the jungle and move from place to place so they couldn't find us. Then a terrible thing happened."

Again, Aunt Mai interrupted herself to pour me some more tea. I think she had to brace herself for what came next.

"We needed food so my family went to a village where we once had some friends. Usually, we stayed away from the villages because soldiers were there and if they saw anyone they didn't recognize, they would follow them back to their hiding spot in the jungle and kill everyone in the camp. The soldiers had left the village a few days before, so we thought it would be safe. Then, that night the soldiers came back. We had just enough warning to run out the back of the hut across the clearing into the jungle. My brother was sleeping in another room and didn't wake up fast enough. Since I was thirteen years old, like you and Vue, I ran the fastest. My mother had slung my little sister on her back. As she and my father were running for their lives, one of the soldiers shot her in the back with a big gun. She fell down, as did my father who had been shot in the leg by another soldier. He lay very still and pretended he was dead. When the soldiers left, my father crawled over to my mother. He found that the bullets had killed both my sister and my mother. We learned later that the soldiers had found my sleeping brother and took turns shooting him for sport.

"My father's leg wound became badly infected and it was now my duty to care for him. Fortunately, with the help of the shaman who had fled with us, I was able to find healing plants that sucked the poison out of his leg, although they could never heal his broken heart. I cared for my father as we moved from camp to camp in the jungle for five years until I was eighteen. Then he died.

"I stayed with the people in the jungle camps. They were my only family now. Then one day, some soldiers came into our camp. They were not the Pathet Laos, but soldiers fighting them. They would hide out in the jungle with us, attack the Pathet Laos, then escape across the border to Thailand. I fell in love with one of the soldiers and we were married. Soon I found I was going to have a

## The Shaman Stone

baby. He promised to help me escape to Thailand, but it wasn't easy. By this time the Pathet Laos soldiers knew who he was. There was a price on his head and he was unable to come across the border for me himself, but after our baby was born he arranged for my escape to Thailand." Aunt Mai got up, walked over to the wall hanging, and motioned for me to follow. "Here is our story," she said. "I have embroidered it on this paj ntaub, as is our custom."

The picture on the paj ntaub showed soldiers with dogs and guns chasing Hmong people across open land and into a river. In the background you could see the village huts on fire. Mai stared at it for a long minute then continued her story. "The river you see on the story cloth is the Mekong River. It flows between Laos and Thailand. We had to cross it to escape from Laos. It is a fast running, deep river and many of our people couldn't swim."

"How did they get across?" I asked.

"Some didn't," said Mai wiping her eyes. "We had to cross at night so the killing guards on the other border didn't see us."

"Killing guards?"

"They were men who were licensed to kill us. We had to be very quiet. Mothers had to give their babies opium so they would sleep. Many of those babies never woke up."

"You mean they died?" I could hardly believe her story.

"Yes," she replied softly.

Without her saying so, I knew her baby was among those that never woke up. I could see that it was hard for Mai to talk about the horrors she and so many others had lived through, but she continued her story.

"The United States government was now supplying some of the aid they had promised, so my husband and I were accepted into the refugee camps. While there, I had a chance to learn English so I helped interpret for the American relief workers. In turn, they helped me look for my sister in the camps, but we couldn't find her.

"Were you safe then?" I asked.

"Oh no," said Aunt Mai. "Conditions in the camps were hard and many people died of exhaustion and disease. The survivors were often robbed by army deserters and other predators. Often the Thai officials who were given money to buy food for the refugees by the United Nations High Commission of Refugees used only part of the money for the refugees and kept the rest for themselves.

"After a while some of the Hmong people were allowed to immigrate to the United States," continued Mai. "My husband and I were among the lucky ones."

"How did you come to live in Maggie Falls?" I asked.

"Many families were sent to live in the unoccupied barracks of the small military outpost near Maggie Falls," she said. "Eventually, some of those families settled in Maggie Falls so they could farm on the river bottoms. Even though my husband and I weren't farmers, we came with them and set up our shop. I had learned to sew and

## The Shaman Stone

embroider when I was little, so that became my trade. We kept hoping that we would find my sister and my nephew in one of the refugee camps and asked the Red Cross to help us search for them. We had almost given up hope of ever seeing them again when the Red Cross notified us that they had found Vue."

Aunt Mai finished the story and again thanked me for being such a good friend to Vue. "I have a present for you," she said handing me a curiously shaped package wrapped in tissue paper.

I opened it to find a small red satin purse gaily embroidered with scenes that were, Mai explained, of their farming village in Laos. It was so beautiful I could hardly stammer out my thanks.

Aunt Mai gave me a big hug and said something to Vue in their language. He dashed up a staircase in the back of the shop that led to their apartment and was down again in a jiffy. With an embarrassed grin he handed me a large envelope with my name written on it in large, perfectly formed letters. I opened it and took out a piece of paper. On it was printed the words "Please come to Hmong festival next Saturday. It will be at Hmong farm outside town. You be my special guest. We will have lots of fun." Vue's face was beaming by the time I'd finished reading his invitation. "You will come?" he asked.

"I wouldn't miss it," I replied.

It was getting late. I knew I'd better start for home if I didn't want to end up walking in the dark. Even though I was in a hurry I couldn't help but be amazed at the transformation of this old run-down part of town. The "cheap rooms" motel had a coat of fresh paint and clean windows. A lot of kids were playing with balls in what used to be the parking lot. It looked like they lived there with their very large family. The tattoo parlor, greasy spoon restaurant, and pawnshop were gone. They had been replaced by a grocery store, a butcher shop, a Hmong restaurant, and even a hardware store with walk behind roto-tillers lined up on the sidewalk outside. I could see gardening tools of every shape and description inside the dimly lit store. I also saw something else I never expected to see in such a place in this part of town—Fred Herrington exchanging cash with the storekeeper for a pair of garden rakes.

# 21

# Back to the Mound

It happened again. Last night I was sitting in my bedroom trying to figure out that page of reciprocals our math teacher had given us for homework when that darn rock started glowing at me. At one time I had thought it might be radioactive so I had checked that theory out with our science teacher. He said if it were radioactive it would glow all the time, not just when it felt like glowing. He said it was probably reflecting a light from somewhere—*or wherever*.

Whether or not it glowed all by itself or by the power of suggestion, it was distracting me from my homework so I picked it up to shut it away in my desk drawer. Big mistake. Almost as soon as I touched it I knew I was a goner—gone from my room and sitting on top of the old Indian mound across the river from the Indian cemetery with the stone clutched in my hand.

The whole place was peacefully quiet. I guess the guards the Indians had posted were away harvesting wild rice with the rest of their people. The rock felt warm and almost alive in my hand. I hung on to it tightly, remembering my first visit to this place when it bopped me a good one and landed me in bed for nearly a week. The rock, locked in my clenched fist, began to pulsate as if it were trying to tell me something. *Listen, listen,* it seemed to throb.

So I listened and in the stillness of that crisp fall night, I heard a faint scraping and thudding sound, not unlike that made by the gravediggers in the Radcliff Cemetery. It seemed to be coming from beneath me.

Again, like that first night, I heard voices, but not the unearthly ones of the times before. These voices were definitely human, but the words were lost in the distance and darkness. What were *they* doing here? What was *I* doing here? As I sat across the river from the graves in the Indian burial ground, I watched the shadows made by clouds moving over the face of the moon as they played over the spirit houses. I wondered how many were shadows and how many were spirits.

My thoughts were interrupted by some very real sights and sounds. I heard the whining of an engine as it was being started, saw the progress of a rumbling vehicle silhouetted against the full moon as it bumped across the decrepit bridge, and watched its headlights blaze a trail down the old Cemetery Road.

# 22

# The Hmong Festival

Saturday was the day of the big Hmong festival. Even though I had been invited personally by Vue the invitation was probably more polite than necessary for at least half the town of Maggie Falls had turned out for the event. Back from a week of wild-ricing many of the Indians were there, ready to enjoy another holiday. I looked for Annie Birdsong, but didn't see her.

The junkyard on the riverbank had been cleaned up. I learned that Pao's family and other families now farming the river bottoms held an open-air farmers' market there on weekends. Today, it was the scene of the Hmong festival. Alive with people, it was a babble of noise-- English, Hmong, the Indian language, -- and, unlike many of the people there, I could only understand the English sounds.

I wished Aunt Betty could have been here to see how neat this mix of people really was, but of course, she has her pride and her suspicions, and worst of all, her prejudices, which all combined to keep her away. Well, at least that Fred Herrington wasn't here, not that he'd come anyway considering how much he dislikes Asians.

Although a lot of the kids from the KWWKers were there with their Hmong KWWKmates, quite a few had decided they had other things to do and didn't bother to show up. Kendra, René, and I had bicycled out to Hmongtown to meet up with Vue and Pao.

"Come," said Vue. "Eat."

He grabbed Kendra with his left hand and me with his right and raced to the nearest food booth with René and Pao following in hot pursuit. There was lots of food: fresh fruits and vegetables --corn, cucumbers, eggplant, beans, onions and melons—all grown in the former junkyard on the river bottoms. We stopped at a food stand and bought some spicy egg rolls, pho, and sticky rice which we ate with relish and a can of pop.

Auntie Mai caught up with us as we sat at a picnic table eating. Dressed in her traditional Hmong costume, she was absolutely spectacular. The knee length skirt was totally decorated with a variety of designs in brilliant contrasting colors—bright pinks, oranges, yellows and greens that sparkled and dazzled. A highly decorated front panel hung like a narrow apron from her waistband to her ankles. She called it a "xe" which she pronounced "shay." On her head she wore a hat that fit like a lampshade and was completely decorated with beads, and the colors and patterns were repeated in her blouse.

Vue and Pao excused themselves to set up the one-game soccer tournament and Auntie Mai offered to show us girls around. She introduced us to some of her friends who were a sight to behold in their native dress. All of the

# The Shaman Stone

costumes were beautiful, but there were differences. "My dress is from the Blue Clan." Auntie Mai explained. "My friend Yer's costume comes from the Black tradition." Yer's black three-quarter length sleeves boasted embroidered patterns, while her friend Vong wore a black blouse with stripes of embroidered cloth on the sleeves with appliquéd flowers sprouting between the stripes. Both women wore heavy necklaces of silver coin that nearly covered the fronts of their blouses. It reminded me of an Indian breastplate I had seen in a museum.

"Yer wears the costume of the Black Clan and Vong's costume is of the Striped Clan," said Auntie Mai. "See those women over there with the plain white skirts? Guess what the name of their clan is?"

"Pink? Red? Yellow?" we teased.

"Oh, now I get it," said René with mock exaggeration, "White."

"Right," said Auntie Mai with a big grin.

"Why all the color names for clans?" asked Kendra.

"It's a strange story," said Auntie Mai mysteriously. "Long ago, when the Hmong lived in the highlands of China, the Emperor tried to divide the Hmong people by making them different. So he named them 'White Hmong,' 'Blue Hmong,' 'Black Hmong,' and 'Striped Hmong' and ordered the villages to adopt different styles of dress, hoping over time they would begin to think of themselves as different people."

"Did it work?" asked Kendra.

"What do you think?" asked Auntie Mai. "Here you see all the different subgroups the Emperor created, but we are still all one people; different styles of dress but shared cultural beliefs."

"What did the Chinese Emperor have to do with it?" asked Kendra. "I thought you Hmong came from Laos."

"We did come from Laos," said Auntie Mai, "and Burma and Thailand and Vietnam, and would you believe long before that, Siberia?"

"Siberia?" I said. "Like the Indians?"

"Yes," she said, "but our ancestors migrated south into China instead of east to the Americas. Then, two hundred years ago, most of the Hmong left China and settled in the mountains of those Southeast Asia countries where nobody else wanted to live. We called ourselves 'highlanders'. We were a separate people but we chose to fight with the Royal Lao army against the Pathet Lao Communists in the 1970s, helping the Americans."

I listened as Auntie Mai related an abbreviated account of the story she had told me for the benefit of Kendra and René.

"Thousands of our people died in the fighting. When the Royal Lao government collapsed and the Americans left, we Laotian Hmong hid in the jungle; then ran for our lives across the border to Thailand. In time many of us Hmong were able to leave the refugee camps in Thailand and settle in America. And here we are," she laughed. "It just took us a little longer to get here than it took the Indians."

# The Shaman Stone

"Yeah," I said. "Like thousands of years."

"Do you know what the word 'Hmong' means?" Aunt Mai asked.

We didn't have a clue.

"Free man. And here at last, we are finally free."

More and more people from town and the Indian reservation were arriving to spend the day at the Hmong festival. I saw Heron and his friends with Pao and Vue, obviously getting ready for the downsized soccer tournament. I thought I saw somebody else there, also, but I couldn't be sure.

Just outside a large white open-sided tent was a sign that read:

> *Ncas: Mouth harp*
> *Thaj Chij: Two string violin*
> *Raj Npliam: Free reed pipe*
> *Nploog: Hmong flute*
> *Qeej*

"Come," said Auntie Mai. "The musicians are about ready to play."

Kendra was studying the sign. "It says," she informed us, "that Ncas will play the mouth harp, Thaj Chij plays the two string violin, Raj Npliam plays the free reed pipe, and Nploog will play the Hmong flute. But what instrument will Qeej play?"

Aunt Mai laughed. "Qeej *is* the instrument," she said. "The sign lists the Hmong name for the musical instrument and its English translation. Except the Qeej cannot be translated into English. There is no other instrument like it."

We went inside the tent which was beginning to fill with people. I noticed that many of the Hmong were wearing red or white strings on their wrists and necks. *Strange costume*, I thought. "Is that part of a Hmong tradition?" I asked Aunt Mai.

The smile disappeared from her face. "It's kind of a tradition," she said. "They wear the colored strings to keep away spirits who might bring misfortune."

"Do Hmong people always tie strings around their wrists?" asked René.

"Only if they have been warned to expect trouble," said Aunt Mai.

I wondered if she was referring to the Granny Shaman's premonition that Pao and Vu had been so worried about.

On the stage the musicians were getting ready to play their instruments, one instrument at a time. First up were a teenage boy and girl. Their hands covered their mouths, but their thumbs kept moving and from their lips came a twanging noise that sounded like talking.

"That's a Ncas. It's like a mouth harp," explained Aunt Mai. "They play it by putting the thin metal blade between their lips. Then they pluck it with their thumbs to produce the vibrations that make the music."

We listened as the boy and girl alternated playing their Ncases. "It helps with the courtship," said Aunt Mai.

## The Shaman Stone

"Clever couples can use the instrument as their own private language."

An elderly gentleman then came on stage to play the Thaj Chij, a two-string violin that looked like a long stick in a barrel with two tuning pegs on other end. He played it with a curved bow that looked more like the kind of bow you shoot arrows with than a bow you play a violin with. But like the musical bow, it was strung with horsehair.

We listened to the free reed pipe that Auntie Mai said was called a Raj Npliam. It consisted of a narrow bamboo tube with six finger holes in the front and one in the back that produced the melodies. It was a lot like the Nploog, or Hmong flute, except it had a brass reed which was inserted into the side of the pipe sliding down the pipe to allow playing.

Then the musician who played the Qeej came on stage holding long bamboo pipes of different lengths that were strapped together and inserted on either side of a hollowed out piece of wood with a tube for a mouthpiece coming out the side. It kind of reminded me of a bagpipe.

"We're very fortunate to have a demonstration of the Qeej," said Aunt Mai. "Sometimes it is played for weddings, and New Year's celebrations, but mostly the Qeej is played for funerals."

We watched with fascination as the musician played the Qeej. Not only did he play the instrument, he danced with it, stepping and bending, turning and swooping.

"It requires a great deal of skill to play the Qeej," said Aunt Mai. "The very best play the Qeej at funerals. They talk to the dead person through their instrument. Their music takes the dead person to the other world. But first the Qeej player must bring the spirit of the dead person back in time to all the places that person lived during his lifetime; back to the beginning of his life here on earth; back to his birth. The music changes with each stop along the way. Only very good Qeej players can do this because they need to play for the right amount of time. If they don't play long enough, or miss a stop along the way back, the spirit will never get to its destination. If they play too long, the dead person will take the spirit of the Qeej player to the other world with him."

At the close of the musical program, an announcement came over the loudspeaker, first in English and then in Hmong, "Ladies and gentlemen. May we direct you to the soccer field where the play-off game between the Red Team and the Blue Team will begin shortly."

As I moved with the crowd, I again had an uneasy feeling that someone who shouldn't be with us, was. I think it was a premonition. I fingered the Shaman Stone tucked securely in its pouch under my shirt. I had taken to wearing it when I was out in public. One could never be too safe.

The soccer field was laid out on a plot of land that had been recently harvested. There was little grass but lots of hard packed dirt with some fresh dirt sprinkled on top that looked like someone had tried to rake it smooth. It

## The Shaman Stone

made for a messy field. I was glad I wasn't playing. The head referee, dressed in a yellow and black striped shirt, short pants, knee length socks, knobby knees, and soccer shoes, was none other than Sheriff Wilkins. I didn't recognize the other two referees. They were probably his deputies.

In the middle of the field a player from each of the soccer teams shook hands to start the game. Rock, paper, scissors determined who would get the ball. The Red Team won. The Red kicker passed the ball to the left forward who took it up the side of the field, overtaking both the left forward and left midfield of the Blue Team. Blue defense knocked the ball out of bounds. Red got the throw-in, pitching the ball high over two Blue defense to his open man. Open man missed and the other Blue defense made a breakaway, kicking the ball into the Red Team's zone. The Blue Team held it in the Red zone, getting a few kicks on net, but the goalie was able to deflect the ball and a Red midfielder picked it up. Two Red midfielders got a breakaway, but after two passes the ball was intercepted by the Blue defense. Defense kicked it up to a Blue forward. Blue forward took it in, kicked on the Red goalie, and got a goal. Score: One-Zip.

The crowd cheered wildly.

Red team got the kick-off and dropped it back to defense. Defense wound up, took a big kick and booted it all the way down to the Blue zone. Blue defense picked it up and tried to pass it to a Blue forward, but the ball was knocked out of bounds by the Red team so they could get a line change. New line came in. Play resumed. Blue forward threw the ball in. It was intercepted by a Red forward who took it up, dribbling around Blue defense and coming in on left side of the net to draw the goalie over. Then he made a perfect pass to the other forward positioned in front of the net.

    The Red forward was just about to kick the ball into the Blue goal net when he stumbled over something and fell. Then we all saw what that something sticking out of the ground was! It looked like part of a bone—a human bone. Sheriff/Referee Wilkins blew his whistle and stopped the game. He went over to inspect what was beginning to look like a crime scene, for it was becoming obvious that there were many more bones covered by the loose soil on top of the soccer field. I had a chance to take a good look at them before they cordoned off the area with yellow tape. I saw bone fragments, big and small, and some teeth-- obviously human. But what caught my attention were the bits of wood with animal pictures inscribed on them that I recognized as pieces of the grave markers Kendra and I had seen on our picnic holiday, and small tubular shaped stones that I recognized from my journey back in time to the Indian village. They were the shaman's sucking stones that had been buried with the victims of the measles epidemic.

    In the confusion that followed, people gathered in little knots talking amongst themselves, trying to make sense of the soccer field turned boneyard. The "mystery presence" also materialized as Mr. Herrington. He was making the rounds, moving from group to group shaking

## The Shaman Stone

his fist and talking up a storm. I noticed, however, that he avoided any gathering with Hmong people in it.

I thought of the dying words of the shaman, *When bone and stone see the sun, the work of the evil one is done.* Bones and stones had obviously "seen the sun" on the soccer field and I had a pretty good idea of who the "evil one" was, but did the words "is done" mean the work was already finished, or is it still being done? And just what is that "work?"

# 23

## Newspaper Headlines

On Monday we headed out to d'Angelos Drugstore to meet the rest of the KWWKers for our usual sodas and to talk over the strange events of the weekend. Maybe it was my imagination, but it seemed as if people were staring at us. They did not look friendly. Not too many of the KWWKers were at the drugstore so there were plenty of booths to choose from. I sat with Kendra and René again but we didn't see Heron or any of the Indian kids. The Hmong kids were talking quietly among themselves in their own language. They looked worried.

Tony d'Angelo seemed nervous. He brought us our sodas and handed me one of those pink "While you were out" phone messages. It was from Aunt Betty. It said, "Please tell Elizabeth Mae Radcliff to stop by my house on her way home." Not too personal, but I was glad she wanted to see me. I had missed her.

I went home to grab my bike and headed out to Aunt Betty's. Each rotation of the bicycle's wheels seemed to churn up another thought of Aunt Betty and Mr. Herrington. What was he to her? Was he her boyfriend? I hoped not, because I not only disliked him intensely, I considered him to be an evil person. He had certainly brought out the worst in Aunt Betty. She believed everything he told her and got mad at anyone who tried to tell her differently. Especially Dad and me.

Aunt Betty opened the door when I got to her house. She immediately shoved a copy of the *Maggie Falls Magpie Gazette* in my face. "See this?" she demanded. "Read it!"

I pushed the paper far enough away so my eyes could focus on the object of her wrath. It was a newspaper article headlined, "Grave Disturbances at Indian Burial Ground." Here is a word-for-word copy of the article.

> *In response to continuing complaints from the Indians on the reservation, Sheriff Ben Wilkens has launched an investigation of the alleged diggings at the Indian burial grounds located north of town. Preliminary findings show that many graves have been disturbed. Bones of the victims of a measles epidemic that decimated the Indian village in the 1800s have been dug up and scattered throughout the site. The disturbance of Indian burials is a federal offense. Federal marshals are being called in to investigate.*

An accompanying article stated that fragments of mysterious bones had been discovered during a soccer game in "Hmongtown." *The origin of the bones is unclear as of this writing,* stated the article. *They are being sent to the state crime lab for testing.*

I'd barely finished reading when Aunt Betty said angrily, "That's what your new friends are up to." Then her face and voice softened with concern. She put her hands on both sides of my face and brought her head close, nose to nose with me. "Elizabeth darling, you can get in bad trouble hanging out with the wrong people."

I was puzzled. "What wrong people?"

"Those people in your KWWK group," she answered impatiently, letting go of my head and throwing her hands up in the air.

"What's wrong with them?"

She looked at me as if I had just arrived on Planet Earth. "Everyone knows what they're up to. It's all over town. They're the ones who've been stealing the Indian bones to grind up for their medicine. And that new pharmacist from New York City is in on it!"

"Who says?" I demanded, although I knew the answer.

"Fred Herrington."

"How come Fred Herrington knows so much?"

"He's a very smart man, Elizabeth Mae. He's been around. He knows what's going on."

"I'll just bet he does!" I shouted. I didn't mean for it to happen, but I was losing my cool. I also knew I had to take a stand. "Aunt Betty," I said trying to keep my voice from shaking, "I'll believe in my friends long before I believe what that creep Fred Herrington tells you. He's just

## The Shaman Stone

a troublemaker! You worry about him, not me!" And I walked out the door.

# 24

# TV Publicity

On Tuesday there was big excitement in Maggie Falls. Early in the morning a large white van with the letters "WMYB" printed on both sides drove up and down all the streets of town and then parked in front of d'Angelo's Pharmacy. A station wagon with the words "News Sensation" splashed on the sides pulled up and parked right behind the van. Some very sophisticated looking men and women wearing a lot of make-up got out of the station wagon carrying pads of yellow paper, pencils, and a microphone. The people in the van wore jeans and T-shirts. They were busy unloading television cameras.

I was on my way to school when I saw them. A lady reporter with bright red lipstick and lots of orangy-red hair piled on top of her head was stopping everyone who came her way and shoving a microphone in their face. She asked a few questions and then didn't ask any more if she didn't like the answers she was getting. She even tried to interview me. She wanted to know if I had heard about the Indian bones that had been dug up.

I said, "Yeah."

"Who do you think is digging them up?" she asked waving the mike in my direction.

"I don't know."

"Have you heard anything about people grinding them up for medicine?"

"Nope," I lied. I knew Mr. Herrington had been telling people that, but I sure wasn't going to say anything about it.

I could tell the lady reporter had lost interest in asking me any more questions because she was looking over my head trying to find a more promising subject to interview. She didn't even notice when I snuck back into the gathering crowd where I hooked up with Kendra.

"What a creep," Kendra said. "That painted lady's just looking for trouble."

"I figured out what those call letters stand for," I said. "WMYB, We Mind Your Business."

"Right on," agreed Kendra. And leaving the bogus news scene, we walked the rest of the way to school together.

That night the "Desecration of Indian Graves in Maggie Falls" was the top news story on TV. The lady reporter, whose name was Marsha Manley, had found the perfect subject for an interview, none other than Mr. Fred Herrington. Ms Manley was practically drooling as the self-described "author, historian and expert on Indian and foreign affairs" wove his tale describing how, "when cultures collide, one culture, namely the Hmong, can trespass on the rights of another culture, namely the Indians', by grinding up the bones of their ancient dead for medicinal purposes."

The City of Maggie Falls was in an uproar after that newscast. A civil war nearly broke out pitting believers against non-believers. A placard army marched in front of d'Angelo's Drugstore with signs demanding the "bone grinding" d'Angelos go back to New York, and then it marched over the Main Street Bridge into "Hmongtown" demanding that the Hmong go "back to where they came from." Rumors flew around like flies about the fate of lost pets, some of which had even been missing long before the Hmong came to town. A few people were certain that they had ended up as "dog meat" on "someone's" plate.

The name-calling continued all week and more demonstrators--many of them new faces that I had never seen before--joined the crowd demanding that the Hmong and the d'Angelos "get out of town." And in the middle of it all was that big white news van with WMYB printed on the side and its star reporter Marsha Manley interviewing the demonstrators, making them feel like celebrities. And, believe it or not, helping Marsha Manley cover the news was her new undercover reporter, Fred Herrington, who was investigating the Hmong community to find out if there were Communist spies amongst them.

The situation got so bad that by the weekend Sheriff Wilkins had to post deputies on the Main Street Bridge to check out people traveling to Hmongtown and back. Our regular Monday KWWK meeting was canceled, so I went

## The Shaman Stone

home right after school. Annie was there sewing jingles on her dress while a pot of stew simmered on the stove. Even though we could hear the demonstrators down the street yelling and chanting Annie acted at first as if nothing were happening. Then she looked up. "Looks like someone's stirring the pot and it's about to boil over."

"Annie," I asked. "Are the Hmong people in trouble?"

"Could be. But then again things aren't always as they seem," Annie observed as she fastened another jingle on her dress.

# 25

# Showdown at the Crypt

The Shaman Stone lay on my dresser. I knew it had something to do with the Indian grave bone robberies. *If only rocks could talk,* I thought. As I watched, it seemed to take on a life of its own—and then a light of its own. It became bathed in a blue radiance that grew stronger and stronger. As if guided by another hand, I picked up the glowing rock and dropped it back into its pouch that was hanging around my neck. In the next instant I found myself inside the wrought iron fence of the Radcliff burying ground. I knew it was cold outside. I could see my breath. But there I was, barefoot and in pajamas, surrounded by a warmth unlike anything I had ever known before.

The moon drifted behind a cloud, yet I could see clearly the objects around me. One of them became brighter than the rest, taking on a bluish glow. I watched as it changed shape and once again I saw my mother. This time, however, I was not afraid. I could feel her thoughts and emotions entering my mind—the joy she had felt bringing a new life into this world, the sadness of leaving her baby girl so soon after its birth. I could sense her love for me and her

# The Shaman Stone

concern for my well being and in that instant, I realized danger awaited me. Not from the ghost of my mother, but from a mortal source.

Once again my mother beckoned for me to follow her. This time I did not hesitate. We approached the massive, padlocked door of the hillside crypt. As I watched, the lock undid itself and the door swung open. Must of the centuries greeted us, but I realized it wasn't Radcliff must. It was much older than the Radcliff burials, perhaps older than time itself.

As the light that was my mother and I entered the cavelike tomb, the stone in my hand began to glow brighter and brighter, lighting up the whole room. Scattered in piles throughout the crypt I saw pottery jars and arrowheads and little carved statues. They were very old. They were very Indian. Some of them looked very much like the objects I had seen buried in the mound when it was so new it was just a bump in the earth. How long had they been in the crypt? Why were they here? And more importantly, who had put them here? Then, in the next instant, I wasn't in the crypt anymore. I was back in my room; back in my bed. But I knew I hadn't been dreaming. I was beginning to think that, as Annie had said, "Things aren't always as they seem." And I began to think long and hard about Mr. Herrington.

The next morning was Saturday. I decided I'd better talk to Aunt Betty about a few things, so I invited myself over for breakfast. The pancakes were cooking when I got there. She seemed glad to see me. I think she had missed me. To my relief, there was no sign of Fred Herrington. When we sat down to eat I asked her how she had met him.

"Wiley Quackenbush introduced us. Fred was here on business. He said he was doing some research for a book he was writing. He also said he was interested in buying some grave sites so I took him on the grand tour of the cemetery."

"Did he buy any?"

"Yes, two lots in Section A. I invited him in for coffee while we drew up the contract."

"Did he pay you for them?"

"Not yet."

"What did you talk about?"

"Oh, this and that. Nothing important."

"This and that?"

"Well, he did seem interested in the cemetery business. I told him how the Radcliffs got started in it. I even showed him the family burying ground."

"Did you show him the crypt?"

"He wanted to see it, but I told him the key was hanging up back in the house. I pointed it out to him when we got back."

"Are you and Mr. Herrington good friends?"

"Now that you mention it, we have kind of a peculiar relationship. I never know when he's coming over. He'll stop by one night and then again the next day. Then I won't see him again for awhile."

# The Shaman Stone

"Aunt Betty," I asked. "Have you ever noticed the key to the crypt missing?"

"No, but then I never pay much attention to it. It hangs right where it's always hung for the last hundred years."

"Well," I said, "I think someone has been using it to get into the crypt."

"Don't be ridiculous, Elizabeth Mae. Why would someone want to get into the crypt? There's nothing there to steal except some old Radcliff bones." Then Aunt Betty got a funny look on her face. "You don't suppose that druggist is grinding them up for the Asian tea market, do you?"

This time it was my turn to laugh. "Don't *you* be ridiculous. Nobody would want the old Radcliff bones. They're too spicy for tea." Then in a more serious voice I said, "Aunt Betty, I think someone is hiding stuff in there."

"What kind of stuff?"

"Indian stuff."

"And just where did you get that idea?" Aunt Betty demanded.

"I just dreamed it up. Let's take a look and see if my dreams are for real."

"Forget it. I'm not traipsing out to the graveyard to check out your dreams."

"Humor me."

Aunt Betty pushed her chair away from the table and walked over to the key rack by the door. A strange look came over her face. "The key to the crypt is missing," she breathed. "Fred stopped by last night." She walked over to the ancient roll top desk that served as her office and rummaged through the pigeon holes until she found what she was looking for, the duplicate key. Holding it in her hand she simply said, "Let's go."

Aunt Betty fit the key into the huge padlock and turned it. The lock snapped open easily, as if being unlocked was an everyday occurrence. The heavy door swung open with little resistance. Aunt Betty gasped when she saw what was inside. So did I. Unlike last night there were no longer piles of pottery and statuettes piled here and there. Today, most of them were neatly packed in boxes and stacked by the door as if they were expecting to go somewhere.

"Omigosh!" was all Aunt Betty could manage at first. She walked inside the crypt and peered at box after box of the grave goods and then at the items still to be packed. "Where did he get all this stuff?"

"I think he's been digging them out of the old Indian mound."

"I don't believe it!" she exclaimed. "He's been using me! And I fell for it hook, line, and sinker!" I could almost visualize a light bulb illuminating her brain as the truth slapped her in the face. *Welcome back from the Dark Ages, Aunt Betty.*

Suddenly I had an awful thought. "Aunt Betty, Mr. Herrington was here last night, but he didn't finish packing up this stuff. When do you expect him back?"

"Right about now," said a voice from outside the crypt. "Sorry ladies, but I'm going to have to lock you up for eternity. With you out of the way, I can come back for this stuff anytime in the not so near future. Maybe I'll collect your bones, too," he cackled, "and grind them up for tea." The heavy door swung shut, and the padlock clicked.

The blackness was fierce. Aunt Betty started to cry softly. "What have I gotten us into," she sobbed. I probably would have joined her for a good cry, but I was too scared. Then the Shaman Stone in the otterskin pouch around my neck started to glow its blue light right through the bag. The light grew and grew, filling the room. In a blue flash the light was gone! So was the inside of the crypt. Aunt Betty and I were standing in the sunlight on the outside of the padlocked door. From the inside came a frenzied pounding and a muffled voice. "Let me out! Let me out!" It was Mr. Herrington. We had switched places!

In another flash we were both back in the house. This time it was under our own foot power. Aunt Betty called Sheriff Wilkins. He was out in no time with his deputies and a carful of federal marshals.

As we walked out to the Radcliff graves, Aunt Betty and I told Sheriff Wilkins what we knew and what we suspected about Mr. Herrington. The guy who seemed to be in charge of the feds looked very interested in what we were saying. He turned to one of the others and said, "I think we've got our man." He motioned for us all to stop before we got to the crypt. He and the sheriff had a short discussion, then they let Aunt Betty and me in on their plan. "We think Fred Herrington is responsible for the looting of Indian mounds all over the country," he explained. "But he's always been two steps ahead of us and we haven't been able to catch him. Until now. With your help."

We continued our hike to the crypt in silence. When we got there, the marshal whipped out a small tape recorder, and each of his men drew his gun. They positioned themselves on either side of the crypt door.

"Oh Fred," said Aunt Betty ever so sweetly. "What on earth are you doing in there?"

"You know very well what I'm doing in here!" he snarled. (Except those weren't the exact words he used.) "You locked me in here you little..." (We'll skip those words, too.)

"Why Fred, why would I do a thing like that?" Aunt Betty had a big grin on her face.

"Never mind!" he yelled. "Get me out of here!"

"How?" asked Aunt Betty.

"With the key, you idiot!"

"But Fred, the key's gone. You must have it."

"Use the other one, dummy!"

"What other one?"

"The one *you* used to open the crypt!"

"But Fred, why should I let you out? You locked Elizabeth Mae and me in there for 'all eternity.' Those were your very words."

"Oh come on, Betty. I was just kidding."

# The Shaman Stone

"I didn't think it was very funny." Aunt Betty was grinning from ear to ear. "Come on, Elizabeth Mae. Let's go shopping."

"No!" screamed Mr. Herrington. "Let me out and I'll make a deal with you."

"What kind of a deal?"

"I'll give you a cut of the profits."

"Profits? What profits?"

"Well, let's call it 'rent'."

"Rent? For what?"

"For the items I stored in the crypt."

"What were the items?"

"Just some Indian junk I dug out of the trash."

"You mean artifacts you dug out of the Indian mound, don't you?"

"No... Yes. Betty, they're worth a fortune on the black market. Let me out and I'll cut you in on the deal."

"Where did the bones come from? Are they worth money, too?"

"No. I had Wiley haul the dirt and bones we dug out of the bottom of the mound along with some bones from the cemetery out to the soccer field in his dump truck to throw everyone off the track and make it look like the Hmong were doing all the digging. Now let me out!"

"Just a minute. I'll have to see what Elizabeth Mae thinks."

The marshals moved to either side of the crypt door while the sheriff unlocked the padlock. He was just pulling it from the clasp when Mr. Herrington came lunging out wild-eyed and disheveled. Knocking the sheriff off balance as he shoved the heavy door open, he headed straight for Aunt Betty and me. "I'll get you for this!" he screamed. He was just about to grab Aunt Betty by the throat when one of the marshals knocked him to the ground and handcuffed him.

    The marshals took Mr. Herrington away with them. I think he was relieved. He knew that jail time was better than crypt time.

# 26

# Sorting It All Out

I stayed with Aunt Betty that night and we had a good heart to heart. At last we could talk without getting mad at each other.

"I'm so embarrassed, Elizabeth Mae. That man played me for a fool and I never caught on."

I knew that was about as close to an apology as I would get from Aunt Betty. She had always had a hard time admitting that she might not "be right" no matter what the situation. She was also trying to figure out what role the Shaman Stone played in our escape, but I chose not to enlighten her on that subject. I doubt that she would believe any explanation I could give her, even if I *could* figure one out.

It felt strange, but good at the same time, to go to sleep in my own bed in my old bedroom at Aunt Betty's house. While I lay there waiting for sleep to come I, too, was wondering about the Shaman Stone. Had it been pure dumb luck that I had seen it in Aunt Betty's driveway and picked it up? Or was there a purpose for it being there. And what about Annie Birdsong? She appeared and reappeared on our doorstep as if by magic. Nobody knew exactly where she lived or how she got from place to place. Was she somehow connected to the Shaman Stone? Was she a part of my adventures in the past?

Early the next morning Sheriff Wilkins came knocking at the door. An Indian man stood next to him. "This is Hank," he said by way of introduction. "He is from the State Archaeologist's Office in St. Paul."

Hank wore work boots, a flannel shirt, jeans, and a long braid hanging down his back. He was tall, muscular, and handsome, about the age of Aunt Betty's old boyfriends. "And these are the two Radcliff ladies," the sheriff continued, "Betty Radcliff and her niece Elizabeth Mae. They're the ones who caught the crooks."

Aunt Betty had never met an Indian face to face. She nearly dropped her teeth.

"Glad to meet you," said Hank shaking hands with both of us.

"Hank has been sent out by the State to identify the stolen goods in the crypt," said Sheriff Wilkins.

"The Department of Antiquities has asked me to catalogue them, also," added Hank. "So I might be around for a while. Do you have some space I could rent here for an office and a workshop?"

Peace came to Maggie Falls with the apprehension of Fred Herrington and his not-too-bright accomplice, Wiley Quackenbush. With their arrest everyone finally realized it wasn't the Hmong who were digging up the graves in the Indian cemetery for bones. It was Fred and Wiley, who were trying to throw everyone off the track while they "mined the mounds" for something much older and much more valuable than bones--the grave goods from the ancient Indian burials. I realized that this was "the work of the evil one" the old Indian legend had foretold.

Of course the story was all over the papers, from Maggie Falls to New York to Los Angeles. It seems that Fred Herrington was a big-time crook, the ringleader of a national gang of grave robbers that specialized in plundering and looting ancient Indian burial sites all over the country and selling the grave goods, or what Hank called "artifacts" on the black market. His activities were so secretive the thefts were not discovered until long after he had disappeared. But this time, thanks to Aunt Betty and me, and some help from the Shaman Stone, they got their man.

According to the *Maggie Falls Magpie Gazette*:

> *Fred Herrington will be tried in Federal Court under the 1966 National Historic Preservation Act. This law makes it illegal to destroy, excavate, or remove any archeological resources from Federal or Indian lands. Under State law, it is a felony to disturb a known burial site.*

Two weeks later another article appeared in the *Maggie Falls Magpie Gazette.*

## June Gossler Anderson

> *Results of the forensic tests performed on the bones recovered from the site of a soccer game held during the Hmong festival have linked some of the bones to the burials of Indian measles victims who died during an epidemic in the early 1800's, as well as to more recent burials. Smaller bone fragments have been found that date back to the first century AD, long before the arrival of present-day Indians. The mystery remains: Whose bones were they?*

I think I knew the answer for I had witnessed the original interment.

The KWWKer's got back together at d'Angelo's Pharmacy & Soda Shop the next week. We had a lot to talk about. More kids than ever showed up this time, and Ms Sutton didn't even have to bribe them with sodas. They bought their own. With the Hmong festival soccer game disaster behind us, we decided that we needed a new project, one that would help restore peace and harmony to our fractured community. Again Pao and Heron came up with an idea. "We're going to collect bones," stated Pao, "and here's the man who's going to show us how to do it."

Heron introduced his guest. "I'd like you to meet Hank. He's been sent here by the State to identify the objects that were stolen out of the mound and to recover the bones that were dumped on the soccer field."

We were all ears.

Hank explained that the Indian bones are sacred to the Indian nation and needed to be re-interred in the ancestral burying ground. "We must do this before the snow flies," he said "or it will be much more difficult to recover them. The larger bones will be easy to find, but the small fragments are very old and look much like the earth to which they are returning." Holding up a small wooden box with a screen for a bottom he continued, "We're going to do this in a professional manner and lay out grids on the field to facilitate our search pattern. We'll start with the outside grids and work towards the middle. Our tools will be small trowels and these sifting boxes to separate dirt from bone. If we have enough help I think we can finish the job in two days over the weekend. Who would like to help?"

Almost every hand shot up.

"Okay," said Hank. "See you at eight sharp next Saturday. We'll meet on the soccer field."

Back at the Maggie Falls Cemetery, Hank and Aunt Betty were working night and day identifying the Indian artifacts that had been stashed in the crypt by Fred Herrington. "Fred Herrington," joked Hank one day when I had biked out, "was a *red herring*. Those bones he trucked out to the soccer field were just a ruse to throw us off the trail of what he really was up to."

Aunt Betty looked happier than I had seen her look in a long time. I had thought at first, when Hank asked to rent office space from her in the old Radcliff house, she'd tell him, "No way!" considering how much she thought she disliked Indians. But, lo and behold, not only did she agree to let him set up shop next to the crypt, she seemed to enjoy his company. And I think he enjoyed hers. Now she had another project to throw herself into; assisting Hank with his work. Since she had never been interested in anything "Indian" before, I was surprised to see that the piles of genealogical books stacked on the kitchen table and chairs, had been replaced by books about everything Indian she could borrow from the library.

Dad and I thought the artifact identification project was very interesting. I biked out to Aunt Betty's every chance I got to help and I was curious to see if I could recognize any of the items from my trips into the past, although I kept that part of my life a secret from everybody but Annie. Annie was often there, too, helping out, and Dad joined us for supper whenever he could.

Outside the crypt Hank had set up several makeshift tables, each one consisting of a door resting on two sawhorses. Pottery fragments lay on one. He was cleaning them with a small brush and trying to fit them together, like a jigsaw puzzle. "The designs on the rim sherds help me to identify them," he said. "If you look carefully at this one you can see the tooth-like impressions that were pressed into the soft clay with a comb-like instrument to make the design. This tells me they were part of the Woodland tradition."

Woodland? Were those the people I had seen burying their dead on top of the bluff so many years ago? "What's the Woodland tradition?" I asked.

## The Shaman Stone

"Woodland is the name given to the prehistoric people who lived in the central United States over two thousand years ago." Hank explained.

"Prehistoric people? Like cavemen?"

"In a way. Some lived in rock shelters but they usually made their homes out of birch bark and hides--homes they could pick up and bring with them when they had to travel from their summer home to their winter home."

In my mind I could picture the people wearing their fur coats paddling their log canoes down the Indian River, and beaching them to set up camp. "What were their homes like?" I asked Hank.

"Like wigwams made of animal skins and birch bark," he replied.

*I know that,* I thought to myself. *I watched them build them.*

"The Woodland people were the ancestors of modern Indians," continued Hank. "We can identify them by their traditional pottery vessels and burial mounds."

Burial mounds--cemeteries. Being the undertaker's daughter I knew a lot about the subject. "How many burial mounds were there?" I asked Hank.

"Over eleven thousand in the State of Minnesota, alone," he replied. "Most of them were round dome shaped hills, like ours, although some were linear-- long like snakes, and some were very large and elaborate, like those in Cahokia, Illinois. Our mound here on the Indian River is among the largest in this state, dating back several thousands of years and containing the bones of thousands of individuals."

"All those dead people!" I said remembering the Indian village. "Was there an epidemic?"

"No," Hank laughed. "The ancient ones buried their dead in the same sacred ground over a period of many hundreds of years, one on top of another, heaping earth over each new burial until a few mounds, like ours, rose over forty feet in the air and would cover half a football field.. However, many mounds were quite small. Just a bump in the earth."

*And to think I knew this mound when it was just a baby.*

"Where are the rest of the mounds?" I asked

"All over the state," replied Hank. "There're mounds at Gull Lake, and Pine City, and Park Rapids." Hank paused to conjure up some more mounds in his mind. "Then there's Malmo Mounds near McGrath, Morrison Mounds at Battle Lake, Blue Mound State Park at Luverne…"

"Aren't there some in the Twin Cities as well?" asked Aunt Betty.

"Yep," said Hank. "Mounds Park in St. Paul and lots of burial mounds in Bloomington and along the Minnesota River Valley. But the biggest one of all is Grand Mound near International Falls."

"When did they stop building mounds?" asked Aunt Betty.

"About the time the Europeans arrived," said Hank.

# The Shaman Stone

"If there were once thousands of mounds, what has happened to them?" I asked.

"Unfortunately, most of them are gone," said Hank. "Plowed under by farmers, dug up for roads, plundered by amateur archeologists, like our 'friend,' Mr. Herrington. That's why laws have been passed to preserve and protect them."

On another table were several varieties of stone and pottery pipes. "Although we're not allowed to excavate mounds anymore," Hank said, "what we have found tells us a lot about the ancient ones' way of life. For instance these pipes show us that Indians in this region traded with Indians to the south for tobacco."

"Do you mean they smoked way back then?" I asked.

"Right-on," said Hank. "Tobacco was very important for their ceremonies."

On the third table lay a variety of items. In one group was a number of, what Hank called, "tooth-edged projectile points," that looked a lot like arrowheads to me. He pointed out some ornaments worn by these ancient people; a necklace made of shells, one made of bones, and one made of bear teeth. "See these hammered-copper breast ornaments?" Hank asked. "This shows that they traded with people in the eastern Great Lakes region where copper is mined."

Stone and bone tools had been placed in another group on the table. Hank showed me a round milling stone used to grind grain; a grooved maul that, when attached to a wooden handle, was used much like a hammer; stone drills, and knives; hide scrapers and a punch used for turning deer skin into clothing. "And this," said Hank holding up a tubular shaped bone, "was used by a shaman to suck illness from the body of a sick person."

# 27

# Celebration

I could hear the music long before we reached the house, single notes some long, some short, clear and crisp, reaching to the sky. Dad said it was "hauntingly beautiful." We had been "officially" invited to dinner at Aunt Betty's house. Hank and Aunt Betty were sitting on the back porch swing waiting for us while Annie Birdsong fixed dinner in the kitchen. Hank was holding a wooden flute to his mouth, his fingers playing up and down the five holes making sounds that seemed to call to the spirits of the trees and the rocks. Aunt Betty had a wooden flute also. "Hank's teaching me how to play it," she said.

When Annie announced, "Dinner's ready," we trooped inside to sit around the big round kitchen table. "We've got a regular Indian feast," she informed us. "Venison from the deer Hank shot, fried bread, squash and corn and blueberry muffins…."

"… and Annie's famous wild rice dish," Aunt Betty added.

We stuffed ourselves with the good food. Between mouthfuls, Dad and Hank kept the conversation going.

"How's your work coming?" Dad asked.

"Good," said Hank. "Betty's been a great help with the cataloguing, and I think Annie knows more about these artifacts than I ever will."

"She's reconstructed some of the pots using the same techniques the ancient ones used," said Aunt Betty. "I don't think you could tell them apart except that her pots are still in one piece."

"We're just about done with the identification and cataloguing," said Hank. "And then there's just one thing left for us to do."

"What's that?" asked Dad.

"Check out the damage those looters did to the mound. I plan to get on it as soon as we return from the powwow. I've been waiting for the trees growing on the sides to drop their leaves and for the brush to die back so we can get a good look at the mound itself without all that foliage covering it."

"In all the excitement I almost forgot about the powwow," said Dad. "Got your jingle dress finished, Annie?"

"You bet. Wanna see it?" Annie disappeared into the back bedroom. In a few minutes we heard her coming out. She was wearing a long, almost-to-the-floor, red and white dress. The yoke was white, embroidered with red flowers and the rest of the dress was trimmed with jingle strips attached diagonally in rows to form Vs. As she moved, the 365 jingles we had made out of tobacco tin tops and sewn to cloth strips swayed and clinked. "What do you think?" she said.

## The Shaman Stone

"I think we've got a winner," said Dad.

"The powwow is next weekend," said Hank. "Betty is coming with me and we'd like the two of you to join us."

"Is Annie coming with us, too?" I asked.

"No," said Annie. "I'll meet you there."

We hit the powwow trail early Saturday morning. By eight o'clock we were at the top of the hill overlooking Duluth Harbor. We could see some ore boats docked along the piers waiting for the railroad cars that ran on the tracks above the ships to begin dropping their loads down the chutes into the open hatches. Looking towards the channel connecting the Duluth/Superior Harbor and Lake Superior, I saw the Aerial Lift Bridge raise straight up and an ore boat leave the harbor. Dad said it was taking its load of iron ore to the steel mills in Cleveland.

As we coasted to the bottom of the hill Dad was muttering under his breath.

"Did you say something?" Hank asked.

Dad looked a little embarrassed. "Oh," he said, "I was just trying to remember the lines to a poem my father was always reciting. I think it goes 'By the shores of Gitche Gumee; By the shining Big-Sea-Water; Stood the wigwam of Nokomis; Daughter of the Moon Nokomis; Dark behind it rose the forest…'."

"Isn't that Henry Wadsworth Longfellow's poem, 'Song of Hiawatha'?" Hank asked.

"I believe it is," Dad replied. "It was a very long poem. My dad liked the part about 'Gitche Gumee,' especially after somebody told him it was the Ojibwe name for Lake Superior. He was kind of mad about it, though, because he had to memorize some of the verses in grade school and his teacher never told him what Gitche Gumee was."

"She probably didn't have a clue," said Hank. "The poem is about Hiawatha and the Indian maiden, Minnehaha, who never existed. Longfellow made her up."

"What?" I said. "I saw a statue of them at Minnehaha Falls in Minneapolis. It was very romantic. He was carrying her."

"Longfellow was a bit confused," stated Hank. "Hiawatha was actually an Iroquois Indian living on the Eastern Seaboard. He never set foot in Minnesota or saw Lake Superior."

Aunt Betty laughed. "So," she said, "all those streets and places in Minneapolis were named after two people who never existed?"

"Yep," chuckled Hank. "A case of mistaken identity. Something like Columbus naming *us* 'Indians' because *he* got lost. However, the city fathers got one thing right."

"What was that?" asked Betty.

"Lake Nokomis. Nokomis was the grandmother of the Indian Longfellow thought he was writing about."

As we drove through Duluth I saw a narrow park wedged in between the street and Lake Superior. Plopped in the middle of it was a weird looking boat-like thing with curled up ends, front and back. Along its sides were round

# The Shaman Stone

painted shield-like decorations and it had a sail and rows of oars coming out the sides.

"That's a strange looking canoe," I remarked.

Dad laughed. "That's no canoe, Elizabeth Mae. That's a Viking ship and this is Leif Erickson Park."

"A Viking ship! How did it get here?"

"It's really a replica," said Dad. "But many people believe the Vikings were in Minnesota about two hundred years before Columbus discovered America."

"How do they know that," I asked.

"They don't for sure," Dad answered. "I think one of the most convincing proofs is the Kensington Runestone."

"What's a 'runestone'?"

"It's a big stone slab with some writing on it. Not writing in an alphabet we can understand, but an earlier alphabet called 'runes'. A Swedish farmer dug it out of his field in a settlement called 'Kensington' near the City of Alexandria in western Minnesota over a hundred years ago. The runes told of an expedition of Norsemen who returned to their camp to find ten of their men 'red with blood and dead'. It's most likely they got this far inland through the Great Lakes waterway. The inscription said they were thirteen days march from the 'sea' which would have been Lake Superior or, as Longfellow called it, 'shining big sea water'," Dad said with a grin. He thought his little joke was pretty funny.

"Isn't the Runestone supposed to be a hoax?" asked Hank.

"Well, the jury's not in yet, and I think there's compelling evidence out there to prove otherwise," replied Dad.

As we drove north out of Duluth, the city began to give way to some very impressive houses built on the lake shore. "Look for the Congdon Mansion," said Aunt Betty. There was a murder there a few years ago."

"There it is," said Hank pointing to a huge stone house with a parking lot off to one side and a graveyard on the other.

"Why does the sign say, 'Glensheen'?" I asked.

"Because it's now owned by the University of Minnesota," Hank replied. "It has considerable historical significance. You can actually tour the house."

"Do they show you where the murders happened?" I asked.

"Yes," replied Hank, "but they don't like to talk about that very much. The house has other importance. Congdon Mansion was built by the richest man in Minnesota, Chester Congdon, who made his fortune in mining. He and his wife, Clara, had seven children and they made this their family home."

"I think some of the family is still here," said Betty pointing to the cemetery. "Is Elisabeth buried there?"

"I think so," Hank replied. "Elisabeth Congdon was the last of the children to live here. She never married but she adopted two children. They think one of her adopted children, Marjorie, murdered her and her night nurse in order to get her inheritance."

## The Shaman Stone

"If I remember right, they put Marjorie's husband in prison for the murder, but they could never pin anything on Marjorie herself," Dad added.

"Yes, it was a tragic ending for the family," said Hank. "Do you know that for the next thirteen miles, all the way to Two Harbors, we are going to be driving on a highway built on property donated to the state by Chester Congdon?"

We drove along the North Shore Drive over little bridges under which flowed streams and rivulets emptying into Lake Superior and saw an ore boat at least a mile out on the lake. I think it was the one we saw go under the Aerial Lift Bridge in Duluth.

At Knife River Hank pulled into the parking lot of Kendall's Smoke House. He got out of the car and reappeared with two smoked whitefish for the four of us to share. Dad and I sat in the back seat taking turns pulling the smoked flesh out of the fish carcass while Aunt Betty popped pieces of the delicacy into Hank's mouth as he drove. When we came to Two Harbors, Hank stopped again at Aunt Betty's (no relation) Pie Shop. We all got out of the car and trooped in to wash our greasy hands and order some blueberry pie, specialty of the house.

"How much further?" I asked Hank

"About 120 miles," Hank replied. "We're going to Grand Portage—almost to the Canadian border. We'll be there in a little over two hours."

We pulled into Grand Portage in the early afternoon. The county fair grounds had been turned into an Indian village. Tents were pitched everywhere. Bleachers encircled a large outdoor ring that had a staging area in the middle for the announcers, the drums, and the public address system. We grabbed some food from one of the many food stands just outside the ring and found a place to sit in the stands while we ate. Hank and Betty sat close together. They were holding hands.

A large number of people dressed in colorful outfits were beginning to assemble at the eastern entrance to the arena. "They're getting ready for the Grand Entry," said Hank. Everyone stood at attention when the color guard came in and began its clockwise march around the arena. They carried the Eagle Staff into the circle, followed by the American, Canadian, Minnesota, and Tribal flags. The flags were followed by veterans from previous wars, and then came the dancers.

"The veterans are revered in the tribes," explained Hank. "They are the flag-bearers and have the honor of retrieving the sacred eagle feathers if they are dropped. Respect for veterans has always been an important part of our culture from the time when the welfare of the village depended on the bravery of the fighting men. To be a warrior was a man's purpose in life. We honor the veterans because they are willing to give their lives so people can live."

After the Grand Entry there was a flag song, then a prayer blessing the gathering. The Eagle Staff, positioned above the American Flag to signify the first nation, was tied to the pole in the center. The announcer called for the drum group. Eight men sitting in a circle responded, pounding a large drum in unison and singing at full blast.

"The drum is thought to have its own powerful spirit," said Hank. "It symbolizes the heartbeat of the Indian nation."

The drum called forth the categories of dancers. Men's Traditional Dancers was first, followed by Grass Dancers, and Fancy Dancers, then the Women's Shawl Dance, and the Jingle Dress Dancers.

"The categories of dancers are based on traditional dances that were once part of spiritual ceremonies, preparation for war, healing rituals, and celebrations of triumph," explained Hank. "Dancers perform clockwise or sun-wise around the arena. Their outfits, or regalia, and their steps let the audience and other participants know who they are and what they can do."

The Men's Traditional Dancers entered the arena. "They're not as colorful as the other dancers," said Hank, "but they are distinguished by their fur-and-feather headdresses. If you look closely you can see the quill-work and bead decorations on their regalia. Some of these outfits have been handed down, father to son, for many generations." The dancers spun to the drumbeat. "See those circular bustles on their backsides?" Hank asked. "They are made of eagle feathers."

We watched the Traditional Dancers swoop around the ring as Hank told us about the dance. "This dance tradition originated back to the time when war parties would return to the village and 'dance out' the story of a battle, and when hunters would dance their story of tracking prey. Traditional Dancers are usually veterans--" Suddenly Hank stopped talking, took off his cap and stood up. The dancers stopped. The powwow stopped. From the four directions of the compass four of the Traditional Dancers descended upon another dancer and gathered up an object that had fallen to the ground, returning it to its owner. Hank explained what had happened when the dancing resumed. "The dancer dropped an eagle feather from his bustle. The four other dancers performed a ceremony to restore the sacred feather's lost power to do good."

"The Men's Grass Dance is next," said Hank. "Long ago the Grass Dancers would be the ones to break camp. They would go ahead of the rest of the tribe to the new camp and dance to mat down the tall prairie grass to make it ready for the families that were to follow." The Grass Dancers, dressed in their colorful outfits with flowing streamers of yarn, looked like wind blowing across the prairies as they whirled and twirled their way around the circle.

The Men's Fancy Dance was colorful and exciting. Dancers wearing double bustles, ribbons and bright streamers of yarn danced wildly, color swirling around them as if each were aflame. "The dancers have to stop

## The Shaman Stone

exactly on the last beat of the drum with both feet on the ground," explained Hank. I couldn't hear the last beats coming for all the noise and excitement, but the dancers could. When the song ended, the arena full of flames was suddenly as still as a winter night, and the crowd erupted with cheers. "Fancy Dancing is exciting," admitted Hank, "but Traditional touches you in your heart, where you are Indian."

It was time for the women to dance. Again, as with the men, the first dance was a Traditional--the Women's Shawl Dance. The women entered the arena wearing colorful fringed shawls over their buckskin outfits and two-stepped their way around the arena.

We could hear the Jingle Dress Dancers before we could see them. This was Annie Birdsong's competition. Hank said that this was the most sacred of the dances; an Ojibwe dance originally used for healing. I watched the dancers perform the steps of the Jingle Dress Dance, moving in such a way that the combined jingles of all the dancers sounded like rain pattering through the trees. It was getting late and daylight was fading from the arena; one by one the dancers fell into shadow, all but one. As if illuminated by a spotlight from within, Annie Birdsong radiated light and danced the healing legends of the Jingle Dress Dancers as if she, herself, had invented the dance.

We waited for the winners of the dance competitions to be announced. Once again, Annie was declared winner of the Jingle Dress Dance competition.

"It's getting late," said Hank. "If we leave now, we can probably get home before sunrise."

Dad and I sat in the back seat half asleep. Hank and Aunt Betty sat snuggled together up front. He had one hand on the steering wheel, the other around Aunt Betty. They talked for a while then Aunt Betty began to cry softly.

# 28

# Discovery

Aunt Betty was still looking sad a few days later when Hank invited the two of us to inspect the Indian mound with him. "Hank's work here is almost finished," she said while we waited for him to get the truck. "This is the last thing he has to do before returning to his office in St. Paul." Then, for the third time in my life I saw my Aunt Betty cry. "Oh, Elizabeth Mae," she sobbed. "I don't want him to go."

Hank drove to the mound along Cemetery Road, the same road Kendra and I had taken on our bike ride so long ago. The ruts I had noticed then were still there, worn even deeper than I remembered them. They must have been made by Wiley's truck as he transported his grisly load from the burying grounds to the soccer field. We passed the Indian cemetery high on the bluff and crossed the bridge to the mound on the other side of the river. Once there, Hank parked the truck and took out his big beam flashlight. We went on foot the rest of the way to the ancient mound. Annie was there, waiting for us.

With the green leaves of summer dried up and blown away we easily found three tunnels that had been dug into the heart of the mound from different directions, all meeting in a large opening in the middle. Sections of cedar poles lay scattered on the ground. Fragments of feathers and fur and human bones littered the area, along with broken pieces of pottery, and beads of shell, stone, and bone. What had been taken out and transported to the crypt had been replaced by heaps of loose dirt, beer bottles and cigarette butts.

"Looks like Fred and Wiley had a busy summer," Hank remarked dryly.

We poked around the hollowed-out earthen room for a while as Hank wrote notes on its condition. Then, the beam of his light picked out an object glimmering in the dirt floor. It was a chain. A very modern looking chain-- and it had been there for a very long time. Annie bent down and gently worked it loose from the rock in which it was embedded. "I think you lost something," she said handing me the golden locket that was attached to the broken chain. I opened it up. Mother's picture smiled at me. It confirmed what I already knew--that I had been here before, long before--at the beginning of time when the mound was new.

"Come with me," said Annie. "I want to show you something."

Leaving the mound we hiked up river a ways until we came to a limestone cliff. Following Annie up a winding path along the face of it we came to a crack in the rock. It looked small, but seemed to grow bigger as Annie

# The Shaman Stone

wedged her way in. We followed her through the opening. Hank's flashlight led us down a passageway into a large chamber. Then it gave out and we were in total darkness. From out of nowhere a light begin to shimmer and then to glow and fill the whole room. It came from the Shaman Stone I still carried in the pouch around my neck. The shadows on the walls of the cavern seemed to come alive, and then we realized they *were* alive! Alive with drawings of bison and bears and wolves that looked like they could jump right out of the rock at us!

"Omigosh!" said Aunt Betty. "Where did all this come from?"

"From a long time ago," breathed Hank. "I think we've discovered some prehistoric art in a very prehistoric cave."

Something else on the cave walls caught my attention. It looked like stick pictures.

"Pictographs," said Hank. "Early forms of writing."

The pictographs looked familiar. I took the Shaman Stone out of its pouch and looked at the markings that glowed on the rock. They were identical to those on the cave wall! *How did that happen? Just how old is this rock? Where did it come from? And the biggest question of all: What am I doing with it?*

I looked at Annie and realized that she was more than a housekeeper, more than a Jingle Dress Dancer even more than a healer and a shaman. I knew then that I had known her before--a long time ago before. And I knew that somehow, in some way, Annie and the Shaman Stone were connected.

Hank, Aunt Betty, and I drove back to Aunt Betty's house. Annie said she would be along later. Hank called his office in St. Paul to tell them of our discovery. They said they would send a team of experts out to investigate the cave. Then Hank drove me home.

Annie was in the kitchen when I walked in the door. She was making dinner. Her face bore no expression. Looking at her no one would ever suspect that we had just discovered a treasure trove of ancient art.

"How did you get back here so fast?" I asked her.

"I flew," she said with a little laugh.

*I think she actually might have.* "Annie," I asked, "how did you know about that secret cave?"

"I've always known about it. Just wasn't its time to be discovered."

"Until now? Why now?"

"Until now," she replied, "much of what Indians hold sacred has been disrespected, destroyed, and looted by non-Indians. But now there are laws in place that will protect our ancient heritage."

"Well, the law didn't keep Fred Herrington from ransacking the burial mound."

"That's because only the spirits knew he was there. That's why they called on the Shaman Stone to protect it," Annie responded.

"And the Shaman Stone called on me to help?"

"That's right. Let's say you were acting as its agent. It showed you the clues, and you put the pieces together and caught the grave robbers--and made the world a better place," she added with a laugh.

"Well, if I was so important, why did it have to bop me on the head?"

"To get your attention," declared Annie. "Even the spirits get frustrated sometimes."

*Those spirits must have been mighty upset*, I thought, *for such a little rock to give me such a big whack.* "Were the pictographs on the Shaman Stone copied from those on the cave walls?"

"Other way around," said Annie. "The Shaman Stone is much older than the writing on the walls. The ancient shamans brought it with them from Siberia on their journey across the land bridge. They copied the message from the Shaman Stone onto the stone walls of the cave to pass down from generation to generation through the ages."

"What do the pictographs say?"

"Truths for the Indian people."

It was time for the big question. I took a deep breath. "Annie, are you an agent for the Shaman Stone, too?"

She paused for a moment before answering my question. "Guess I am," she said quietly. "From the other side. I'll return there when my work here is finished."

I think I had already guessed that. I took the Shaman Stone out of the otterskin bag hanging around my neck and held it out to Annie. "What am I supposed to do with this?"

"You'll know when the time comes," she replied.

Hank called in the experts from the State Office of Archaeology to investigate our discovery in the limestone cave. The experts called in more experts and, after extensive testing, they all agreed that the cave paintings and pictographs dated back to the earliest beginnings of man in the State, some eight thousand years ago. They explained that thousands of years ago the Indian River was a shallow stream flowing level with the floor of the cave. At the end of the Ice Age the rushing waters of the glacial melt cut through the limestone, hollowing out the cavern. The current cut the river channel deeper and deeper over the years leaving the cave entrance high and dry and hidden from sight.

The experts declared the cave and its ancient artwork to be a major archaeological find and recommended to Congress that it be placed on the list of National Historic Sites. The State then decided that such an important pre-historical site deserved recognition and a bill was introduced in the State House to allocate funds to build an interpretive center.

Not to be outdone, the Indian community agreed to build an Indian museum and allow the recovered artifacts to be part of the exhibit. And even the Founding Families of Maggie Falls got into the act. They commissioned Aunt Betty to write a history of the early peoples in our area,

## The Shaman Stone

which would be for sale in the museum bookstore. (She asked Annie and me to help her. She knew that we were experts in that area.)

Hank was put in charge of photographing the original cave paintings and supervising the building of a replica of the cave that would be constructed on the site of the exhibit. He said that access to the ancient limestone cave itself would be prohibited to the public to protect it from looters, vandals, and deterioration. (According to the scientists, even people breathing in the cave could help destroy the pictures; it had something to do with exhaling carbon dioxide.)

Instead of returning to St. Paul to do his work, Hank kept his office at Aunt Betty's to prepare for the opening of the interpretive center and Indian museum complex.

Aunt Betty was in her glory, helping Hank. Except for the times we got together with Annie to work on the book, she was usually too busy to pay much attention to me, but I didn't mind. She and Hank had become more than just working partners. They had become friends--and more than just friends, I suspected. And I had my own friends, Kendra, René, Heron, Pao, Vue (who was talking English a mile a minute now), and the others from the KWWKer Club. I was in seventh-grade heaven.

One night in spring Aunt Betty and Hank invited Dad and me to dinner. Annie was there as well.

"How's the building project coming?" Dad asked by way of conversation.

"Great," replied Hank. "The plans are almost finished and we break ground this spring. I'll be supervising the construction and when it's completed I'll have a new job. The State has appointed me to be the museum curator."

"Congratulations!" said Dad. "Does this mean you'll be staying here in Maggie Falls permanently?"

"It does."

"Then will you be moving into town or staying on the reservation?"

"Neither," said Aunt Betty with a big smile on her face. "Hank and I will be living right here in the old Radcliff house. He's asked me to marry him."

Epilogue
# Flight of the Eagle

It was a cool, partly cloudy spring day. As guests of the tribal elders Dad, Aunt Betty, and I accompanied Hank and Annie Birdsong to the mound on the bank of the Indian River. The water on the surface of the river was as smooth as glass--not a breath of wind anywhere. At the base of the bluff the spiritual leaders performed a purification ceremony. The boxes of bones that had been recovered by the KWWKers from the Hmong soccer-field gardens were carried up the winding path to the top of the ancient mound with Annie Birdsong leading the way. The elders placed the bones and offerings in a large hole that Hank had dug in the mound for this purpose. I added one more item to the burial--the Shaman Stone.

    Those of us assembled in that place circled the burial hole placing handfuls of dirt in it along with sacred offerings of tobacco. Annie Birdsong stood apart from the group, partly hidden in the mist. As Hank took his flute from its leather bag in preparation for the final prayer, a tremendous gust of wind suddenly blew in from the river. Annie smiled at me then disappeared in the mist and wind. In her stead appeared a bald eagle. It took flight and soared over the group gathered below. The wind and river became completely calm again, and we stood in awe, motionless and silent for many moments before resuming the ceremony.

June Gossler Anderson

# The Shaman Stone
Bibliography

## Indian Prehistory/History/Culture; Mound Builders & Shamanism

**Works Consulted:**
Michael K. Budak, Grand Mound, Minnesota Historic Sites Series published by Minnesota Historical Society Press, St. Paul 1995

June D. Holmquist: "The Grand Mound," Minnesota's Major Historical Sites

Elden Johnson, The Prehistoric Peoples of Minnesota, published by Minnesota Historical Society Press, St. Paul 1988

Kay-Nah-Chi-Wah-Nung Historical Center, The Place of the Long Rapids, Stratton, Ontario

American Indian Studies Department, University of Minnesota, and the Educational Services Division, Minnesota Historical Society, The Land of the Ojibwe

John A. Grim, The Shaman, Patterns of Religious Healing Among the Ojibway Indians University of Oklahoma Press, 1983

Jesse D. Jennings, "Across an Arctic Bridge," <u>The World of the American Indian,</u> National Geographic Society, 1974.

Peter J. Mehringer, Jr. "Weapons of Ancient Americans" National Geographic, Vol. 174, No. 4, Oct. 1988.

Michael D. Lemonick and Andrea Dorfman "Who Were the First Americans?" Time Magazine, March 30, 2006, p. 44-52.

Michael Parfit, "Powwow, A Gathering of the Tribes," <u>National Geographic,</u> June, 1994

Internet: American Indian Culture Research Center: "The Powwow and its meaning"

Internet: "Antiquities Laws and Regulations" http://cc.msnscache.com/cache.aspx?q

Wikipedia: "Shamanism"

**Places visited:**
Indian Museum, Mille Lacs, Minnesota
Kay-Nah-Chi-Wah-Nung Historical Center, Stratton, Ontario
Grand Mound, International Falls, Minnesota
Powwow, Grand Portage, Minnesota

## Hmong

**Works consulted:**
W.E. Garrett, "No Place to Run: The Hmong of Laos," National Geographic, Jan. 1974

Spencer Sherman, "The Hmong in America," National Geographic, Vol. 174, No. 4, Oct.1988.

Science Museum of Minnesota: "From China to Minnesota: A Brief History"

Science Museum of Minnesota: "Animism and the Shaman"

Internet: Hmong Cultural Tour; "Introduction: Journey Back to Laos," "Refugee Experiences," "Sue Bassett on Refugee Camps"

Internet: "Hmong Culture": http://www.laofamily.org/culture/culture_infor2.htm

Internet: "Bayview: Hmong Music, Food, Shaman," http://csumc.wisc.edu/cmct/DaneCountyTour/madison/bayview/bayviewmusic.htm

Internet: "The Hmong in Minnesota" (Excerpts) by Yang Dao http://cc.msnscache.com

## The Shaman Stone

Internet: ArtsNet Minnesota: "What Is Art? Thailand (Blue Hmong)"
http://www.artsconnected.org/artsnetmn/whtsart/hmong.html

Internet: "Hmong carving out a new landscape along the Snoqualie," Thursday, October 5, 2000 by Phuong Le, Seattle Post-Intelligencer Reporter
http://seattlepi.nwsource.com

Internet: "Learn About Hmong-Free-Reed Pipe"

**Interviews:**
Ker Lor whose story of escape from Laos is incorporated into *The Shaman Stone*.

**Places visited:**
Science Museum of Minnesota, Hmong exhibit
Hmong Cultural Center of St. Paul

### About the author

June Anderson has lived in Andover for over half her life and has been writing for most of it. Combining her love of history with her love of writing, she is a contributing writer for the history columns in the ABC newspapers. Her hobbies and passions include grandchildren, gardening, genealogy, and ghosts. (She conducts Ghost Tours in the City of Anoka May through October for the Anoka County Historical Society.)

You are invited to visit her website:
www.grannygirlpress.com